The Women of Janowka

Helmut Exner

The Women of Janowka

A Volhynian Family History

English translation by
Gabriele Goldstone, Sascha Exner
and Ken Steinke

Dedicated to

Frieda Steinke
(1930-2021)

Bibliografische Information der Deutschen Nationalbibliothek
Die Deutsche Nationalbibliothek verzeichnet diese Publikation in der Deutschen Nationalbibliografie; detaillierte bibliografische Daten sind im Internet über **http://dnb.d-nb.de** abrufbar.

The Women of Janowka

2nd edition 2021

ISBN 978-3-96901-028-0

Dieser Titel ist auch als eBook erhältlich
in den Formaten ePub und Kindle.

picture credits:
Cover: Katlika with her daughters Frieda and Evelyn
(family archive Darlene Omichinski)

Portrait of Helmut Exner © Ania Schulz
as-fotografie.com

editor & dtp:
Sascha Exner

Publisher:
EPV Elektronik-Praktiker-Verlagsgesellschaft mbH
Obertorstr. 33 · 37115 Duderstadt · Germany
Fon: +49 5527/8405-0 · Fax: +49 5527/8405-21
E-Mail: info@epv-verlag.de

Preface

Since the first edition of this book I have been receiving many letters from readers from all over the world. People whose families had to find a new home feel the need to tell me about themselves. Since many of the descendants from such families no longer speak German, an English-language edition of the book was required, which again resulted in new readers and even more letters.

The descendants of relatives who had lost touch from each other over the decades also came forward. In the age of traveling and fast communications, one can track down one another again even after generations. Contacts and visits across continents have become a matter of course and a great enrichment.

Home is not necessarily tied to one place, but something that you can take with you wherever you go. And family is like a tree with many branches and twigs growing in different directions, yet the roots remain as one.

Duderstadt, Germany
October 2021

Helmut Exner

Prologue

Where is Volhynia?

A couple of years ago, when I started to delve into my past, I found myself asking this question. It is a region with a poignant history in the northwest corner of Ukraine. Above all, its history was poignant for the people who once had lived there. Several generations of my forefathers were born there, got married, had children and were buried in Volhynian soil. Everything changed, however, with the generation of my grandparents. If I tried to establish contact with my relatives now, I wouldn't have to travel to Volhynia, because there's nobody left whom I'd know. The people who once lived there are scattered about the continents, and have started new lives. The descendants of the former German Volhynians, to whom I also belong, can be found everywhere but in Volhynia. Today, those who once considered themselves Volhynians, are Germans, Poles, Americans, Canadians, Australians, Brazilians, Argentinians...

Nevertheless, something has remained which, unconsciously, has been spreading itself from generation to generation. The values of the multicultural and multireligious Volhynian society. These values include trust in God, tolerance and multi-lingualism. Astonishingly, even after a hundred years, common things like eating habits and an attachment to the rural life are found amongst the descendants.

My story begins in Volhynia. To be honest, it's only a minor part of *my* story, but, above all, it's the story of four outstanding women, namely my great-grandmother Christine, my grandmother Serafine and my great-aunts Mathilde (Katlika) and Martha. These women were the ones who took our family's destiny in their hands and showed them the way into a new life. Without their courage and their energy, this family would no longer exist.

Volhynia 1904

– 1 –

"Friedrich, get out of the water! You're supposed to deliver the butter to the Jew."

Ten-year-old Mathilde stood on the bank of the small river to bring her brother home as her mother had instructed. After a hard day working on the field, black-haired and wiry-slender Friedrich, eighteen years of age and the oldest son of the Exner family, had waded into the almost dried-out river to cool down, along with the other boys and men. The water level was too low for anyone to consider swimming.

"Turn around then, I'm coming out now. Or do you want to see your brother in the nude?"

The girl put her hands in front of her face, while the other boys made deriding catcalls.

Their parental home, a rather simple, but solid stone building, was only about 200 meters away. On the ground floor, there was a spacious kitchen and a small parlour. A precipitous stairway led up to three bedrooms.

"Well, have you washed your dirt away in the river?" asked Christine, the mother of the family, while she prepared dinner at the stove. "Take the horse and ride over to Solomiak, so that young Salomon gets his butter. Make sure he pays you today. The month is over and I'll find a good use for that money."

"Why must I ride to Solomiak? Isn't Gottlieb here yet?" Friedrich countered.

"He's still at the Hinzes. He might be late since they're mowing today. Come on, please go now. Remember, once you're back, dinner will be waiting for you."

Gottlieb was Friedrich's sixteen-year-old brother. He was helping out their neighbours at the moment. The father of that family had fallen off a horse a few days earlier, and was still recovering. Beside Friedrich, Gottlieb and Mathilde, Karl and Christine Exner also had eight-year-old Martha. Several children had died early.

The Exners made their living off the land, like almost everybody else in the small German village of Janowka by the river Slusz. Christine, the undisputed head of the family, which of course no one expressed loudly, was a woman in her early forties, dark-haired, small and thin, with brownish-green eyes which could look directly into one's soul. She was a brilliant organizer assigning all the family's work, even that of her husband Karl (without him noticing), and administering the housekeeping money. When the – mostly Jewish – grain merchants or cattle dealers came into town, she would determine the deal by either nodding or discreetly shaking her head at her husband. Aside from the housework, she looked after the cattle and the big garden, assisted with hay-making and the grain. Thus, she made it possible for her husband to earn a bit extra as a craftsman. They did not have a hard life.

Of course, there were also poor people in the area. There were poor Germans who – like anywhere else in the world – could never get off the ground. There were poor Ukrainians, Poles and Russians who weren't able to seize opportunities with both hands, even after serfdom had been officially abo-lished in 1861. And, of course, there were people just living from hand to mouth. Some families had no choice but to live in mud huts.

Anyone who could no longer work due to poor health, and had no family to support him would be in a bad situation. The most effective social net was a big family which also included more distant relatives. Of course, the parish was res-ponsible for charity and neighbours were always there with practical help. But for effective and lasting support, one counted on one's family. Therefore, it wasn't surprising that often whole clans either emigrated entirely or little by little. Almost everybody in the village had a large number of relatives in the area which constantly increased through marriage.

People considered themselves first as Volhynians, and then as Germans. Volhynia, located in the northwest of Ukraine, had been Polish for a long time. In 1792, after the third Polish division, the Russian Tsar took over the region. His subjects, however, didn't have much reason to complain. As early as the 19th century Germans had already settled here. Immigration increased in the 1860s, as many of the former serfs had run away from their landowners. Nevertheless, there were only a few willing to work as farmhands, because this they could do in Germany. Those who came here wanted to be their own masters, no matter how small the piece of farmland was or how hard one had to work for it. There was nothing the big landowners could do but lease or sell vast pieces of their land. Besides, there was still much land waiting to be broken. Settlers cleared the land and drained the swamps. All this made the Tsar regard his new subjects with great favour.

Volhynia bloomed with the arrival of the many German colonists in the 1860s and onward. The economy flourished. In the bigger towns, there were all kinds of tradesmen and also the first industries, and, of course, a lot of shops that offered everything one's heart desired. Houses were built and had to be furnished enabling carpenters to earn their daily bread. Cloth was needed to sew clothes, which gave business to the textile manufacturers, who, in turn, required raw material from the farmers. Everybody needed clothes and footwear. Tools were required. Production and trade was booming. An optimistic spirit ruled.

While prosperity in this province grew, bitter poverty was prevelant in many other areas of the gigantic Russian empire. This phenomenon, however, when many people enter a thinly populated area, get settled and boost the economy, had been already known in Russia for centuries – for example, in the Volga region or in the Black Sea region. In 1890, there were about 2.5 million Germans living in the Russian tsardom, 240,000 of them in Volhynia. Of course, Germans were not the only ones who had come from faraway to live here. Driven by the desire to build a new and better life in Russia, people from many other countries were setting off. Apart from Russians, White Russians, Ukrainians, Poles, there were also Dutchmen, Czechs, Slovaks, Lithuanians and Hungarians attracted to Russia. In addition, they were joined by several single adventurers from many other countries who were also longing to achieve some degree of prosperity. Numerous people who were victims of religious persecution in their home countries, had come here, too. Religious freedom had been granted to Mennonites, Hutterites, Baptists and others.

The immigrants had an inspiring influence on the whole empire, but then things changed. Tensions grew between the Tsar and the German emperor. Many privileges the Germans had been given were suddenly cancelled. These privileges included the freedom from taxes, the exclusion of military service or the right to speak German at school. Under the rule of Alexander III the lives of Germans as well as other minorities in Russia gradually got worse. Jews, in particular, were despicably treated. In the Schtetls there were certain Jews who were doing well, some even very well, but most Jews were facing bitter poverty. Under Tsar Nicolaus II the situation worsened. To add to this, unrest was growing within the Russian population. Both the autocratic rule of the Tsar and the privileges of aristocracy were defended with an iron hand. After the revolution of 1905, an informer network, with the intent on exposing politically conspicuous persons, was installed. A careless remark made under the influence of alcohol could be enough to send one to a Siberian penal camp.

– 2 –

Friedrich was on his way to Solomiak, riding on his bay with an easy canter. As usual, when he was on his own, he was completely lost in thought, not even noticing the farmsteads and fields he was passing. Instead, he wondered whether he'd meet some representatives of the opposite sex in Solomiak. Indeed, there were two or three girls he'd already had his eyes on for a while. But what was he going to do if one of these adorable creatures crossed his path? Come to an abrupt halt?

He slowed his horse to a walking pace. *Well, if one of these girls comes my way now, I can start a conversation without appearing too pushy. Women! What a cross to bear.* Those who were his age just wanted to get married or else they had pushy parents who were just waiting to marry them off at the first opportunity. The fifteen or sixteen year old girls weren't a good choice either unless one was willing to run the risk of getting a beating, with a flail in the worst case, by some infuriated father. If, against all odds, one succeeded in getting close to a girl out of the public eye – and something happened – then one had to get married anyway. No – he still loved his freedom too much. For this reason alone he was just happy to have escaped from his grandfather's family.

Otherwise, he'd presumably eke out his existence weaving at some loom. Some of his cousins down in the Dubno area had been working in the factory of his Uncle Robert. Others, particularly the women in the family, had a loom at home working until they became deformed. That was no life for him. Thank God his father was a farmer. The land up here was big enough to share with his brother Gottlieb one day – all the better, if they'd get the chance to buy some extra acres. If his parents hadn't taken the initiative to come here, he'd probably have also ended up working in the cloth factory. *Over my dead body,* he thought. *Moreover, I'm still too young for marriage and children.* He was completely surprised when he had suddenly reached his destination, which rudely awoke him from his thoughts.

"Sholem-aleykhem, Salomon."

"Ah, Friedrich, mayn friend. Ikh have already thought, du would nit kum mer or ze puter haven nit become thick enough in this weter."

Once a week, young Salomon came to the Solomiak colony collecting butter from the local farmers which his parents sold in Kostopol, the chief town of the district. He was about thirty years old, a bearded man who had been very popular with the people in the area, being friendly to everyone and always cashing up correctly.

For centuries, Jews had been banned from farming and/or carrying on a trade almost everywhere in Europe. Therefore, most of them had been specialising in trading. Salomon's family had been dealing in butter which was essential for preparing kosher meals. Sometimes he would even send Jewish milkers to the cowsheds to ensure that everything was kosher. Christine did not allow this, so Salomon, at the very least, put milk buckets at their disposal which were not to be used for anything else. His customers could have complete confidence in getting genuine kosher butter and his suppliers always received their money on time.

Thus, Salomon's family had achieved a modest degree of prosperity over the years. Salomon was married and had four children. His parents as well as some other older members of the family depended on his work. Salomon was fluent in several languages. His Yiddish accent, however, always came through, especially when he used Yiddish expressions which, upon closer examination, had already been known in many other languages and, consequently, weren't regarded as typically Yiddish. Because he was getting around a great deal, visiting various villages and colonies and returning back to town in between, he'd always been a steady source for news. Usually, the villagers looked forward to his visits hoping to catch on up his news, though a lot of what they got to hear these days was far from good. But many people just kept on nurturing the hope that bad things wouldn't reach them.

"Well, Friedrich, here's dei dough far ze month," said Salomon counting out the agreed amount quietly and carefully on the small table which he had put up beside his carriage. Then he made a note of it in his cash book and asked Friedrich to sign his full name. As every Thursday, Salomon had his two span carriage standing in front of the barn of a farm in Solomiak.

"Well, what's the news?"

"There is nothing new. Heaps of work, as always."

"Have du hert already that ze Schindels have sold, too?"

"What?" uttered Friedrich completely outraged.

"But where are they going then? There won't be a bed of roses waiting for them in the German Reich either. That's for sure."

"Who's talking of Deitschland?" countered Salomon.

"Canada! That's a big country in America, to the north of ze United States. It belongs to ze Engelish Queen, who appears to be thankful far every new immigrant willing to turn the wilderness into farm land. People have been telling amazing things about Canada. Ze few British living zere aren't able to take ze cold winters, nor do they cope with ze hot summers. But ze likes of you, young and eager, being used to clearing land, working on the field in the heat and chopping wood in the freezing cold, it is exactly richtik."

"I'm not gettin' it into my head. One can't just drop everything and start all over again."

"It's not as bad as getting nothing for it some day, and – on top of that – getting shot in the Tsarist army. Just have a look at the Mennonites. First, they were promised that they'd not have to join the army, now the Tsar has been calling up all ze young fellows. By ze way, many Mennonites have already gone to Canada. They've even founded a town over zere: Steinbach. And, from hearsay, they've been doing pretty well."

Silence spread, and was then interrupted by Salomon.

"The Tsar wants to bring everything under Russian control. My foter still remembers it, when ze village you live in, once was called Johannesdorf. And what's it called today? Janowka! In Deitsche and Polish and Ukrainian schools children have to speak Russian, everybody has to serve in the Russian army. If you don't obey zere orders, they either revoke your lease contract or ze bank no longer gives you a loan. So, either you become more Russian than ze Russians or you become poor as a church mouse slogging as someone's vassal."

"Up to now neither your family nor mine has become impoverished. Butter is always eaten," Friedrich replied with a smile.

"As long as you're still able to afford it. Just think about it, mayn friend. I've been hearing quite a lot, but most of it is not good. There's something brewing in Europe. My cousins travel from ze Black Sea coast to Hungary, from Poland to ze Deitsche Reich. Ze only thing that matters to ze emperors in Austria and Deitschland is power.

They don't care about ze common people – ze farmers, ze workers or even ze Jews – they show as little concern as ze Tsar."

At this moment, a farmer's wife came by with another butter delivery, so the chat was over. Friedrich said good-bye, mounted his horse and rode away.

"See you next week."

Salomon shouted: "Give your parents my regards!" Then he turned to the woman with a smile.

– 3 –

"You're so pensive today, Friedrich. Didn't you enjoy the perogies?" asked Karl, the father of the family, after the mother and both girls had already left the supper table.

"I've been thinking about what Salomon told me today."

"Good heavens! That Salomon... he's just like his old man. Is the world coming to an end once again? Or has lightning struck his loo?"

"There's always a grain of truth in what Salomon tells," interjected the mother from the other end of the kitchen.

"He said the Schindels have also sold their property and will emigrate to Canada," said Friedrich.

"What?" shot out of Karl's and Christine's mouth simultaneously.

"Well, life hasn't been easy recently, but as far as I can remember it's always been like that," said Karl with a mixture of excitement, defiance and grief.

During the last few years, many German, but also Polish and Ukrainian farmers from the region, had sold their land and belongings. Several Germans had moved to East Prussia, many others, however, had gone overseas. Over the last few years, there had been a lot of talk about Canada. In Kostopol and Tuczyn there were posters in different languages calling for people to emigrate to Canada.

"Nevertheless, one can't just abandon everything that's been built with great difficulty and sacrifice," said Karl. "We've just moved up here a couple of years ago from Kopan, because there's more and better land here for us. In a few years you can be your own master, and Gottlieb too. What do you reckon life was like where your mother's father came from? He was living in Poznan, laboriously building a life for himself and his family, as his father and his grandfather had done before him. Because the Germans had not taken part in the Polish national uprising, it became more and more difficult. They simply didn't want to have Germans there anymore, especially no Protestants. Over and over again, there had been use of force. One day, my father-in-law, like many others, packed up the wagons and came here to Volhynia with the entire family. Of course, it hasn't been easy here either. You know the land we used to have in the Kopan area wasn't properly nourishing our growing family. Therefore, we have come to this place. Well, my boy, thing's aren't too bad here, are they? Moreover, your Uncle Robert has turned your grandfather's small weaving mill into a respected cloth factory."

"Of course, this is wonderful," replied Friedrich who felt himself being taken seriously when his father talked to him like that. "I'm just telling you what Salomon told me. But, somehow, I have a feeling he's right, after all. And the Schindels were right, too, with their decision to go to Canada. Recently, more and more Germans have been put into the Tsar's army for four or five years military service. Many can't get a loan from the bank anymore to buy land, and leases aren't extended. Sometimes I have the impression they want to drive us out of the country."

"Rubbish!" roared Karl. "Volhynia, the whole of Ukraine, even the entire tsardom has been dependent on us. Catherine the Great was only too pleased to get Germans into the Russian Empire. Even us, although we've arrived much later, have done good work and have received many privileges in return. So, why should things change? Everything will remain the same. Believe me! We have our German churches and schools. This is the only place in this huge empire where everybody can read and write. There are Germans in the Russian administration, there are German officers in the Russian army. We're the ones who make sure there's no famine – what reason should the Tsar have to drive us out of here?"

The longer he talked the more furious Karl became, while Christine sat down again at the table trying to appease.

"Fair enough, Karl, but please be a little more quiet."

Karl was a grumpy man – at times – always expressing his views loudly and backing up his arguments with abrupt gestures. Sometimes he would pound the table with his fist causing the plates to jump. Those who didn't know him would no doubt get scared. As far as his family and the neighbours were concerned, however, this kind of behaviour was absolutely normal. It was just Karl as they knew him. When he would get angry with his sons because they were fooling around, he'd loudly announce what was in store for them, as soon as he'd get a hold of them. Sometimes he yelled a warning to rub some bacon rind onto their bottoms while he cut off a rod from the hazelnut shrub and threateningly waved it around. If, after some time, they dared go near him again, his anger would have fizzled out, and nothing would happen. At the most, he would take them by the ears and say: "If you do this again, then may the Almighty help you!" No doubt Karl himself once had a head full of silly ideas, so it would seem unnatural to him if his sons had been different. It would only get dangerous when he became quiet. But that rarely happened.

Karl had a distinctive sense of humour the more crudely explicit the better. He wasn't afraid of making a respectable person, like the local teacher, the butt of a joke. Once, when the pastor had visited a town meeting, he had given high praise to the teacher for doing a good job, and his breast was swelling with pride. Karl's loud comment was: "Well, Richard, all you need is a plume of feathers up your arse now, and you'd pass for a peacock." Christine wanted to sink into the ground, while the entire community snorted with laughter. The pastor said in his loud voice: "This is Karl as we know him. Without his comments we would be poorer." Indeed, nobody ever held that against him, as everybody knew that Karl was a good-hearted soul. Whenever someone needed help, he was there, giving a helping hand without asking questions. Like the rest of the family he wasn't very tall, but he became broader over the years. He could still carry a beam alone, which his sons could only manage together.

Christine was the exact opposite of her husband, a rational person. What she said was well thought-out and carried a lot of weight. The children did what she asked. Karl believed that his wife had been blessed with extraordinary intelligence. When she asked him to do this or that, he sometimes replied: "Yes, Sir!" And if one of their friends made an ironical remark saying Christine seemed to have everything under control, he said in response: "I am the man in the house. What my wife says will be done." *At least someone in the family must be sensible,* thought Christine. If her husband wasn't able to completely get rid of his childish nature, it was her job then to maintain some order in their everyday routine. Still, she loved him for who he was. For nothing in the world would she want to have a grouch or a tyrant in the house. One always knew where one stood with Karl. He always freely said what he was thinking.

Today, however, Karl had become a little pensive pondering over what his son Friedrich had said. The day's work had been done, and he was sitting in the garden behind the house. *Damn and blast* – he thought, *everybody can't just take off. This has been going on for years now. Come what may – I'll stay where I am. A man my age can't just give everything up and start over, whether in Germany or in Canada or elsewhere. With nothing.*

After a while, Christine came over from the house, giving her husband a pat on the shoulder, saying: "Don't you worry too much. There's always a way. It'd be best if we go in now and you have a good night's sleep. Tomorrow morning everything will look completely different, I'm sure. We have to get up very early."

"As every day," answered Karl.

Canada 2008

– 4 –

In almost every family there is, according to genetic disposition, an accumulation of distinguishing physical features: hair colour, height, posture, striking noses, dark or light skin, freckles, big or small feet, fat or slim. Of course, the whims of nature play a role in deciding whether maternal or paternal features dominate in each particular child. But family traits go beyond the mere physical. There are also certain characteristics, qualities, attitudes and likes or dislikes, which are grouped in many familes. One can say "the love of horses is in his blood." or "good cooking runs in the family", but such qualities are probably based on family traditions and upbringing. Nevertheless, it is truly astonishing when after a hundred years, despite being separated from a family who was scattered throughout the continents, one comes across these same character traits, attitudes and likes and dislikes.

This is exactly how I felt when I first met the descendants of my family who had emigrated many years ago. On my father's side, people have always been rather small. Dark hair, grey-green-brown eyes and a dark complexion have been unmistakable indicators of a family connection. For generations, there's been a tendency to have the small finger of the right hand shorter than that of the left hand. This is cause for a good laugh when this or that cousin meets for the first time. Many women in the family have been of such petite stature one should never have thought they had the tenacity and strength required to bring up the many children, drive a team of horses over a field, care for their parents and grandparents and, if necessary, assert themselves against all men. For a long period of time, this family has been living and surviving because of the very power of these small, inconspicuous, thin, tough women.

I had exchanged some letters with Aunt Frieda and talked to her on the phone a couple of times. Her English is perfect, and the East European German she learned from her parents is fair. I already knew her oldest daughter and youngest son from their first visit to Germany. I was immediately attracted to them because they were both petite and dark-eyed. And, of course, cousin Darlene also has this 'magic little finger'. Even more agreeable to me was the fact that both, despite their modern academic professions, were connected to the land and surrounded themselves with horses, cats and dogs, grew tomatoes and potatoes, and enjoyed the company of a big family – brothers and sisters, granny, parents, grandchildren and a confusing number of cousins. It was exactly this lifestyle I knew from my father and it defines family for me.

And now the first meeting with Frieda in Manitoba, Canada. She's a small person, and although at the age of 78 her hair is grey, she's unmistakeably a dark type, loud, full of energy and warm-hearted. The embrace is long and firm. Frieda – a daughter of the petite Mathilde who, in 1904, had brought her older brother (my grandfather) home from the river in Volhynia, so that he could deliver the butter to Salomon, the Jew.

Volhynia 1910

– 5 –

In 1910, there were about sixty houses in Janowka which, to a vast extent, were located on the river side of the road, overlooking the fields which reached towards the horizon. In front of the houses, there were flower gardens. In the back, people had their stables and barns and, of course, big vegetable gardens. A stone's throw away, the river Slusz flowed peacefully. It only flooded occasionally in spring. A small ferry, operated by a Frenchman, crossed the river, enabled the villagers to make hay on the eastern meadows and return it to their barns later on. The parish hall and schoolhouse in which the sexton and his family lived was at the end of the village. On Sundays, a service was held there, led either by the sexton or the elder parishioner. The pastor lived in Tuczyn and was responsible for 56 parishes. He visited most villages only twice a year and conducted school inspections and confirmations. He also signed baptism and death certificates. The baptisms and funeral services themselves were led by the sexton or other parishioners. In order to get married, most couples travelled to Tuczyn, which – going by horse and carriage – was a journey of several hours.

From Janowka, at that time, there were about forty children attending school, joined by some others from the adjoining Janowka colony, which consisted of a handful of farmsteads. There were also some pupils from the Solomiak colony which was two kilometers away. All Protestant children were required to attend school for six years in Volhynia. This rule was common only in Volhynia and in some Mennonite colonies in the Black Sea area. Most people in the extensive Russian Empire were illiterate. Summer and autumn holidays were comparatively long, because parents depended on their children to assist them in working the fields. The basic aim of education was to teach children reading and writing, so that they could read the Holy Bible. It was regarded as a matter of course that this knowledge could also be used for other interests. Arithmetic was also taught, plus more, depending on the educational level of the teacher. Not being a qualified teacher, the sexton ran a tight ship, teaching forty to fifty children of different ages within the confined space of the one-room school. In the 90s of the 19th century, however, education had been taken out of the hands of the Evangelical Church and now teaching Russian was mandatory. German lessons were only permitted between eight and nine o'clock in the morning. Since the Russian administration didn't have enough Russian teachers at its disposal, they hadn't been too stringent about these rules, at least not in the villages. Besides, people learned Russian, in addition to Ukrainian, Polish and Yiddish through practical application in day to day life.

There were German, Ukrainian, Polish, Russian, Mennonite and Jewish villages. There were bigger places with a mixture of many nationalities and religions. All mingled together and respected each other's differences.

Almost all inhabitants were farmers, and many also plied a trade on the side. There were some who had one main occupation and did no farming; like the blacksmith, the miller and a few others. Every home had a stall, a barn, and a garden for fruit and vegetables. In the morning, the cows of the village were picked up by a herdsman, who supervised them during the day while they grazed on a centrally-located pasture beyond the village. In the evening, he drove them back to the village, and without requiring too much attention, every cow would find the way back to its home stable. Some fields and meadows were situated a long way from the village. Every family worked for itself, but helping each other out on a mutual basis went without asking. Some men worked in more distant towns and returned home only on Sundays. Anyone who worked in Shitomir, could come home only rarely, but usually earned good money.

It was only in the last decade that much of the land had been wrested from nature and made useful for agriculture. Beside pastures, corn and potato fields, there were fruit trees. The fruit that couldn't be preserved was made into fruit wine or distilled into schnapps providing a welcome source of additional income for many people, even if it was unlawful. Distilling licences were expensive. People were self-sufficient, producing their own butter, cheese, meat, fruit, vegetables, and flour for bread. In case there was lack of something, one could always swap with the neighbours. The flat landscape, with trees bordering the fields, could be described as pleasant. Summers were hot and sometimes dry; winters could get freezing cold when the wind was blowing from the east.

"Katlika, don't let mother catch you," shouted Friedrich watching from his garden as his sister Mathilde, whom everybody just called Katlika, disappeared quickly in the direction of the river with 18-year-old Eduard Ehmke.

But the 16-year-old girl, who, because of her size, could be taken as twelve, just waved cheerfully. She was certain that her big brother would not tattle on her. Of course, mother Christine had strictly forbidden her to hang around with boys. However, this didn't have any effect on the fact that she was in love. The riverside with its reeds was the perfect hideout for lovers, offering them a chance to talk to each other, or do whatever young lovebirds usually do, without being disturbed by the looks of others.

Half a year ago, Friedrich had married Serafine, the daughter of Pauline and Karl Rattai, who lived in the two kilometer distant Solomiak. With her blonde hair, she presented a nice contrast to Friedrich who, like all his brothers and sisters, had full dark hair and a dark complexion. Serafine, a wonderful singer, was helpfulness itself, getting along well not only with her parents and brothers and sisters, but also with her husband's family. Thus, Friedrich felt he had won the lottery with her. Serafine's forefathers on the mother's side originally came from Mecklenburg. Living in Poznan from 1760 on, they had been faced with increasing difficulties, like most Germans living among the Polish majority, until they decided to come to Volhynia about 1860 trying their luck here. The family of her father once was Sorbian, had also lived in the Poznan area long ago until they, finally, had come to Volhynia, too.

Friedrich had seized the opportunity to take over the farmstead of a family that had moved to Königsberg, East Prussia. Having saved some money himself, his parents as well as those of Serafine had pooled all their money in order to make the purchase of the property possible for the young couple. On instructions from the authorities, the bank in Kostopol no longer granted loans to Germans even if they had Russian passports. However, Russian citizens couldn't be stopped from buying a house, of course, if they paid for it in cash.

Friedrich's parents, Christine and Karl, lived only a few houses further down the road. His brother Gottlieb would take over their farm sometime in the future. The two girls, Katlika and Martha, would have no trouble getting into good marriages since they were both so diligent and clever. Although they were small and thin, they had learned how to be a good farmer's wife from their mother. Moreover, by now the girls were much prettier than their parents liked. They had to constantly supervise and make sure the young men didn't go anywhere near them.

"I'm riding over to Solomiak," said Serafine, as she came out of the summer kitchen, a small separate building used for cooking during the hot season.

"Oh right, today's Thursday and Salomon is waiting for his butter," replied Friedrich.

"I'm also dropping by the parents' place to get some bread. Mother baked yesterday."

"Would you like me to harness the horse?" asked Friedrich.

"I'm able to do it myself. I'm a big girl already, you know," answered Serafine, smiling.

– 6 –

Please, Lord, let me be pregnant, said Serafine half to herself and and half to God while she led her one-horse carriage over the dusty road to Solomiak. Up to now, she had been living a settled life. Her passions had been singing and reading. Two years ago a certain young man came regularly to Solomiak and started besieging her like a cat would approach hot rice pudding longing for the moment when no one was watching. Since then, she'd discovered her third passion – Friedrich. They had either met secretly or pretended to just run into each other on the road. Of course, her parents noticed what was going on. *But why ever not?* mother Pauline thought. *Friedrich is a good boy from a respectable family. He'll have his own farmstead some day, and Serafine will make a good farmer's wife. She could work hard without complaining.* One day, Friedrich, all of a sudden, was invited into the house by her parents, since they wanted to take a closer look at him and his intentions.

"You've been coming to Solomiak quite often lately, Friedrich," said the father, Karl Rattai. "I guess business keeps attracting you here, right?"

"Not only."

"Well, what else then?"

"Well, there's a girl of whom I'm very fond."

"Ah, a girl. Would you tell me who that girl is?"

"Her name is Serafine and she is your daughter."

"You must be joking, boy, just like your father. But that's exactly what I like about him. It appears you've picked a few things up from him. If you're working as hard as your father, I don't mind if you and Serafine make plans for a future life together. You are thinking about the future, aren't you? Or are you just interested in a short pleasure?"

"No... I mean yes, of course, it's about building a life for ourselves."

Finally, after having talked to his parents, too, the Rattais took Friedrich into the family as a fiancé while Serafine was welcomed by his parents as a daughter-in-law. When their plans to get married advanced, both families met and gave some financial support, so that the young couple could take over the farmstead of an emigrant. Neither family had been poor; and besides, property was cheap at the moment because there was plenty up for sale.

Feeling more than blessed and contented to finally be sharing a life with someone she loved dearly, all Serafine needed to make her happiness complete was a 'bundle of joy'. If she had interpreted all indications correctly, she was indeed pregnant. What a tingling feeling! Hence, she had been in good spirits when she noticed Salomon busy at his milk wagon.

"Any news from Kostopol, Salomon?" asked Serafine, after she delivered her butter.

"Ze times are gradually getting worse wherever du may look. Life has become miserable in ze schtetl and even in ze villages folks complain more."

"Oh Salomon, stop always painting things so black. I know things haven't been going too well. More and more people are leaving."

"It smells of war. Ze deitsche emperor's been rattling ze sabre. Ze Austrian has been struggling to hold his empire together. And ze Tsar has been dragging more and more young fellas into his army. If I didn't have to care far ze Mischpoke, far foter, moter and aunt, I'd go to America."

"Well, Salomon, we can't just all leave. It's good that you stay here. Otherwise, from where would people get their butter?"

Today, Serafine wasn't in the right mood to listen to Salomon's pessimistic words. She didn't want anything or anyone to spoil her hopeful thoughts. Now, Salomon was even talking about war.

For God's sake. Let me just get out of here quickly.

"Anyway, I must go now. Please say hello to your parents from me, Salomon. Your father used to come here often in the past. But I haven't seen him for ages."

"Ze parents have bekum old. Still, they run zere store from early in ze morning till evening."

Serafine headed her carriage towards her parents' farmstead. Her brother Rudolf, a young man of marriageable age, was just coming out of the pigpen, waving at her and then escorting her to the house where Mother Pauline was waiting for them in the kitchen.

"Well, how are you doing, my girl? Are you still happily married? Let me have a look a you." She took her daughter by the shoulders and looked right into her the face. "Well, you're looking good. I think, it's going to be a girl."

"But Mother, how on earth do you know what's going on with

me? I'm not sure myself yet."

"Believe me, it's true. You'll see! It would be a miracle if a woman from our fertile family was not pregnant yet after half a year of marriage. At least, this is something pleasent. Everything else is terrible."

"What is so terrible?"

Her mother took a letter from the kitchen cupboard, sat down at the table and started to read out loud, until tears suffocated her voice. Her oldest daughter who lived a day trip away in another colony had fallen seriously ill not long ago. They gathered from the letter that she had worsened. Serafine just sat there, as rigid as a statue, while her mother said in her slightly recovering voice: "I have to go and see her – come what may. I know she has a good mother-in-law doing her utmost to care for her, but I believe she really needs me now. Oh God, I've been worrying myself sick about her. What's happening to my child?"

All of Serafine's joy, after her mother had confirmed her suspected pregnancy, was gone. *Goodness me, Justina, why don't you give me a sign when you're in such a bad way? I can't stand the thought something is happening to you and I can't be there to help you. Such is life then – joy and sorrow have always been close companions.* She set off for home feeling sad and pondering the turn of events. It hurt her to see her mother cry and Justina's illness weighed on her mind. She always had a close relationship with her sister.They'd been kindred spirits since they were little girls and could communicate with each other without saying a word. They had often enjoyed themselves by reading each other's thoughts. Later, things developed so that one girl knew when the other was in trouble. When Justina married and moved away, both sisters agreed on 'letting each other know' when something 'happened'. There was no need of any more words, as both were aware of how that would happen and, of course, that it would work, too.

When she arrived at home, it was suppertime. Serafine cut the fresh bread which her mother had given her into slices and put lard, sausages, cheese and cucumbers on the table. Then she called Friedrich who had just finished milking the cows to come in.

After grace Serafine said: “I think, I’m going to the parish hall later on to attend choir practice. Actually, I don’t really feel like it with this marvellous weather. But I have to take my mind off something.”

“Why? Isn’t it enough if you just think of me?”

“Today, I’m afraid it’s not enough. My sister has gotten worse. I have a very bad feeling.”

“Okay, then go and sing. I’m having a bath in the river, and later on, I’m going to try the beer you brewed.”

Despite the warm summer’s evening, on which most people would rather rest in their gardens from the day’s hard work, the parish hall was well visited. There were several women but only a few men from the village, two women from Solomiak as well as the young Ukrainian woman who had been staying and working with neighbours all summer long. The sexton was the choirmaster. People sang German, Russian, Ukrainian and Polish folk songs. Every singer had a handwritten songbook containing all the lyrics. Because only a few were able to read music, hardly anybody had taken the effort and time to transfer the notations from the sexton’s sheets.

Meanwhile, Gottlieb had picked up his brother Friedrich to go to the river with him. In order to enjoy this evening properly, they had each taken along two bottles of Serafine’s beer.

“This is the life!” said Friedrich. The two men sat on big rocks by the river and had each started on their seond bottle of beer. They still hadn’t dressed. Because they rarely drank alcohol, the beer was having its effect. Both became livelier and more boisterous. Then Gottlieb waded into the half dried-out river and slung a handful of mud at Friedrich.

“Damn! You’ll get that back!”

He ran behind Gottlieb and did his best to also sling mud at his brother. When all was said and done, both looked like ghosts from outer space.

“Mud is healthy,” said Friedrich while he kept on loading himself with mud, until only his eyes poked out of the grey-brown mire. Gottlieb copied.

“Serafine should see us like this. That would be heaps of fun.

Imagine, she enters the house and we rush down the stairs roaring and grunting like wild boars," suggested Friedrich.

Hardly able to control their laughter, they went into action. When they reached the house, the mud on their bodies had already dried. They expected Serafine to return home from singing any moment, so both men went upstairs to hide. It wasn't long before they heard somebody open the front door. Making the most terrible and harsh noise, Friedrich slowly went downstairs, followed by his brother Gottlieb. It took a few seconds until they noticed that in the kitchen – apart from Serafine – there was also their mother Christine as well as the sexton's wife. All were paralysed by fear and unable to believe what they were seeing. It was the sexton's wife who first started to scream hysterically, followed by Serafine. Christine was the first to recognize that these muddy creatures weren't monsters but her sons.

"You maniacs!" she shouted.

Serafine's screaming turned into chuckling, while the sexton's wife yelled with rage: "You blasted guys! One should give you a proper thrashing. I almost died. Look at you! You're prancing naked before women. Shame on you!"

"But we're wearing mud suits," snorted Friedrich with laughter, still gasping for air.

"Off with you! Wash yourselves and get dressed!" interrupted Christine with a mixture of indignation and convulsions of laughter. "I'll tell your father to give you a good hiding."

"I doubt that. If he knew what fun this was, he would have joined us for sure," shouted Gottlieb, as he ran out of the back door.

And he was right about that. When Christine and Gottlieb told him about the incident later on, Karl said to his son: "Why didn't you let me know about your plan? I would have given something to see that silly horse face of the sexton's wife."

"She is such a nice woman," said Christine.

"I'm not saying she's not a nice woman. But her face looks like a mare that's being serviced by a stallion."

"Karl, oh Karl, you will not change any more in your life. It's not a mystery why your sons can never think of anything sensible. As if I hadn't been punished enough with such a husband, I had to get another two sons who are the spitting image of you."

And since Karl always needed to have the last word, he answered: "The fruit of the womb is his reward..." After a short pause he added: "As arrows in the hand of a mighty man, so are the children of youth."

Christine was speechless, while Gottlieb chuckled to himself about his father's words.

– 7 –

Later, when the young couple was lying in bed, Serafine still giggled while Friedrich burst out laughing from time to time.

"You have to stop making me laugh so much, Friedrich. That's not good for a woman in my condition. My belly still hurts."

Now it was out. Friedrich jumped out of the bed roaring: "What?"

"I think I'm pregnant. I've missed my period now for the second time. And my mother said to my face that I was expecting."

"This is awesome. I'm becoming a father."

"Yes, a father of a daughter."

"I don't mind having daughters, especially if they are like you."

"Oh, you're oozing charm again."

"Sure. I don't have anything against a son, by the way. But we're still in the beginning of our endeavours. We can still have lots of children. The most exciting part of it all certainly is the endeavour of making them."

"Tonight, however, there is no need to try it any more. It has already worked. It would be best if we try to sleep now."

"What a pity. But tomorrow is another day – and another night."

Serafine didn't have a good night. Several times she was torn from her sleep by bad dreams. Though she couldn't remember properly, everything revolved around her sister.

The next day was again hot. Serafine and Friedrich were in the field turning over the hay. In the neighbouring field Gottlieb and his mother were busy doing the same work.

"I hope the Ukrainians come tomorrow, so we can bring in the hay," said Friedrich.

Every year, especially at harvest time as well as when hay was made, Ukrainian farm hands would come to the village to assist the farmers who could not deal with all the work on their own.

"They'll come. Aljoscha has promised to come with his two boys. His wife won't make it in her condition."

It was not yet midday. But in the shimmering heat, everyone was already bathed in sweat. Not a cloud in the sky, not a breath of wind. Then – all of a sudden – an enormous clap of thunder, followed by a prolonged rumble. Serafine was thunderstruck, literally, her blood ran cold. After the strange noise was over, Friedrich and Serafine looked at each other. This couldn't be thunder! Not with weather like this. Cannons? Possibly war had broken out without anybody having noticed it... No. Where would these cannons be located then? One could look out to the horizon. There were no cannons. Then loud music could be heard as if an orchestra had started playing nearby. In the meantime, Christine and Gottlieb came over from their field gazing at the others in bewilderment.

"What's this? Where is the music coming from?" asked Christine.

Gottlieb said: "Did you hear that thunder? I don't believe it."

"I do," answered Serafine. She *knew*.

Germany 1962

– 8 –

There are more things between Heaven and Earth... what things? Things that cannot be explained? Things that seem to come from the supernatural? Things that can only be regarded as incredible? Things that should not exist or happen according to the laws of natural sciences and logic? But, nevertheless, they are real. *There are more things between heaven and earth* is a saying which I've often heard. Because in my family, these *things* have been occuring over and over again for generations.

In 1962, I was a nine-year-old child. One day, when I should actually have been at school, I was staying at home lying on the sofa for whatever reason – maybe, I was ill indeed or didn't feel like going to school. I don't know anymore. However, a car stopped in front of our house. My mother was looking out of the window to see who got out of the car and her face took on a trance-like expression. After long seconds had passed, she said quite slowly: "I think it's Aunt Natalie."

I think it's Aunt Natalie. If she had said: "I think it's the man from the moon", it would have made no difference to me. To me, Aunt Natalie had always been some sort of myth, someone beyond reach. Born in Volhynia, she was the sister of my father and had been living in the GDR (German Democratic Republic) which, at that time, used to be called Eastern zone or the East. My parents had not seen her for more than twenty years. My mother had stricly forbidden my father to travel into the Eastern zone. It had been known that, in 1945/46, the Soviets had taken several people, who originally came from the Ukraine, back to the Soviet Union. Since then many hadn't been heard of ever again. Apart from that, GDR citizens hadn't been allowed to travel into the West. However, it truly had exceeded my wildest dreams to personally meet Aunt Natalie. To me, she was like a fairy tale figure, a dear aunt, who had been there once and then had been living at a place so distant as to be beyond reach. Now, this aunt had been allowed to travel into the West. Due to a serious illness, she had become a pensioner, although she had not reached retirement age yet and never would. Aunt Natalie was a small and thin little person of inconspicuous appearance but with a huge heart. She told the story of her mother Serafine:

On a hot, cloudless summer day in Volhynia, Ukraine, her parents experienced this phenomenon of thunder during glorious sunny weather and hearing the sound of music without any orchestra playing. Soon after, Serafine went to her house, packed a few things, harnessed the horse and picked up her mother, setting off for her sister who had *let her know*. After staying with some relatives for the night – everywhere in the area, there were people with whom they were related or were friends with – they finally reached the house of their brother-in-law and son-in-law. It was no surprise when, with sad faces, they were told that Justina had *gone home* at the very same time that the thunder had rolled and the music had played. In our family, one didn't die, one went home.

Volhynia 1912-1913

– 9 –

Serafine and Friedrich had their first daughter, Auguste, in February 1911. In October 1912, Natalie, their second daughter was born. A few days later, baptism was performed by the sexton. Since Serafine needed some time to recover from the birth, 18-year-old Katlika had been helping her with the housework in the last few weeks. Having to cope with two little children took some getting used to. And the house and yard work didn't get done on its own. Katlika, however, enjoyed being with Serafine and the little girls. Moreover, she thereby was able to divert her thoughts, since she had fallen in love.

What had begun as an ordinary crush for Eduard Ehmke two years ago, had in the meantime become a great love. If only she could marry Eduard at once. Her father Karl, however, was of a different opinion. She could still pass for a thirteen-year-old girl, was small and thin, so that her father didn't want to admit that she had become a grown-up and marriageable young woman. Some time ago, he even gave Eduard a talking-to, and said to him: "Now listen, son. As long as you're not married, make sure you keep your hands off my daughter, as well as your other body parts. When Katlika is old enough and you still like each other, you can come and talk to me and I'll be ready to listen to you."

The problem was that Eduard didn't know when Katlika would be old enough in Karl's mind. Other girls already got married at the age of seventeen, or even earlier in case one was expecting. Katlika had been pestering her father at every opportunity. In this matter, mother Christine would have the deciding vote anyway – as always. If she said to Karl that Katlika was old enough to marry, then he would readily agree.

Katlika sat in Serafine's kitchen working on the butter churn. In her mind she held an inner monologue which was a mixture of fury and disappointment.

What is Father thinking? I'm not his little girl any more. I'm a grown-up woman. Just because I'm not a big, fat matron, it doesn't mean he can treat me like a child. Damn it all! I just want to do what everybody does, lie in the same bed with a man, get touched everywhere without having to push him away ever again, nor putting him off indefinitely. I want to be alone with him. I just want to have my fun! And Mother? She's just like him! I can't hear it anymore: Wait a little bit longer! You are still so young, and Eduard is still so young. It's always the same old story and it's getting on my nerves!

"Well, Katlika, just by looking at how energetically you've been working on the butter, I'd say it's done already," said Serafine.

"Wow – you really gave me a scare! I've been completely lost in thought. And I am furious."

"Obviously! You must have love problems."

"On the contrary. I would like to finally marry."

"I think, I should talk to your mother. Why shouldn't you get married at your age? Besides, Eduard is a nice guy. And if you marry him, we'll not only be sisters-in-law, but will also be related to each other, since Eduard is a cousin of mine."

"Is there anybody in the area to whom we aren't related?" asked Katlika.

"Well, there aren't too many, that's for sure", replied Serafine, smiling.

"Well, talk to Mother then, please do. I can't stand pushing Eduard away any longer for fear something could happen. But if it happens – against all odds – it'll end in disaster."

"Well, we won't let it go that far. I promise, I'll talk to your mother at Christmas when everybody is going to be in a good mood. And if your mother says 'yes', then your father can only nod his agreement."

Both women had to smile which ended up in rambunctious giggling.

On Christmas Eve it started to snow. About six o'clock in the evening the entire village flowed to the parish hall. Usually, a service centred on the sermon and readings from the Scriptures. But on Christmas Eve there was singing, too. The choir, which otherwise performed on the occasion of burials, had rehearsed some songs. Most parishioners had to stand, since the few chairs were reserved for the aged and infirm. With great fervour, the sexton said a prayer whose truthfulness nobody doubted:

"Lord, let us furthermore live together in peace and harmony with our brothers and sisters whether they are Germans, Russians, Poles, Ukrainians or Jews. Preserve all of us from need, hunger and war. Protect the Poles and Ukrainians, too, who live in our village and are not here tonight because they have another religion."

The sexton expressed just what everybody was thinking, since in the past few years certain segments of the population were increasingly at a disadvantage. The Poles had been suspicious of the Russian authorities because they had been regarding this land as theirs. And so it had been for centuries – until the Russians, in the course of the third Polish division, had annexed Volhynia as part of their empire. The fact that so many Germans lived in this region, annoyed the Tsar even more intensely. In his opinion, the Germans should live further east which was less densely populated. Since Volhynia was located not too far from Germany, he was also having the enemy in his own lines in case of an armed conflict. To emphasize the Tsar's request, the Russian administration was instructed not to allow any people of German origin extensions on expired leases, nor were banks allowed to grant them loans for buying property. Hence, more and more families were leaving the area. Some had moved eastwards, many had gone to East Prussia, some had emigrated to South America, but the vast majority were starting a new life in North America.

Things weren't going well for the Ukrainians either. Until 1861, many of them had been serfs – first under Polish and later under Russian rule. As a result, most of them never had the chance to own a piece of land in their own country. So, the emigration of Ukrainians, to Canada in particular, was huge. Since 1861, when the big Polish landowners found themselves having no more serfs cultivating their vast fields, farmland was either sold or leased. Since many Ukrainians were too poor and could never afford being their own masters, Germans flocked into the region, mainly escaping from the chaotic situation in Poland. Up to the turn of the century, hundreds of German villages and colonies were founded. Before that, there were already some German settlements which had been founded mainly by Mennonites who had come from West Prussia. Many of them used to have Dutch and North German names, as their forefathers had come from Friesland where they, like in almost any other German region, had been persecuted because of their religion. There were Ukrainian, Polish, Russian, White Russian, Lithuanian and Jewish villages. A big patchwork rug consisting of old and new settlements in which people worked for their own good as well as for the public good of the country and, thus, turning Volhynia into a significant breadbasket of Europe. However, all of this was in danger now. Black clouds were gathering. The rulers of Europe had their own points of view. Apparently, they hadn't been interested in the public good, but in their own well-being.

Confronted with this background, most people did not succeed in enjoying Christmas as much as they usually did. Many families had been decimated. How could one take pleasure in the holiday roast while the children and grandchildren were in America? Probably, one would never see them again. So, Christmas had a slighly bitter taste, leaving more and more families with mixed feelings of grief, pain and tears. Besides, there had been a lot of talk about an impending war. That simply was beyond the power of people's imagination. And how could that happen in the first place? There was literally no one who wanted war, not here in Janowka and not in the villages around either. However, everyone was aware that there were things over which they had no influence. In order to do so, one would have to penetrate into the minds of the high and mighty.

At Christmas 1912, the Exner family in Janowka was not yet reduced by emigration. With the help of a few glasses of wine, they succeeded rather well in taking a more lenient view of politics and, of defusing the danger of war.

"Oh what a nice Christmas that was!" said Christine to her husband when they were sitting together in the parlour.

"True, there is nothing better than having many around livening the place up," agreed Karl.

"However, I feel sorry for Robert. This time, he certainly had a sad Christmas," Christine mentioned, having become rather thoughtful. Robert, a brother of Karl, had been living further south in Berestetschko, a town belonging to the Dubno district. where he had been running his cloth factory. Four of his sons, however, had emigrated to Canada this past year.

"Yes, but there's nothing you can do about it. If the young folks have decided to go this way, one cannot tie them down."

"I know," said Christine, while she topped up her cup with tea. "We have been spared so far. We only have four children, and everyone should be able to make a living here."

"The question is," said Karl taking his glass of wine from the table, "whether in the future anyone here will still be able to make a living."

– 10 –

"Well, my boy, heave your bottom onto the sofa and listen to me," said Karl when he and Eduard were alone in the parlour.

It was a few days after Christmas. Friedrich and Serafine had talked to mother Christine who then had finally made up her mind to allow Katlika to get married. Of course, Karl had persuaded himself that it was his decision. So he talked insistently to Eduard.

"I have talked to Christine, and we both agree on allowing Katlika to marry next year."

A cold shiver ran down Eduard's spine and he went red in the face.

"It goes without saying that you must take good care of her. Though you're still a very young bloke, you can work hard, I'm perfectly aware of that. We have brought Katlika up to be a tidy and diligent girl who will be a good wife to you. So, you better be good to her. Don't make me break every single bone in your body. We can set the wedding after Easter. Until then you will have to control yourself."

He winked conspiratorially at his future son-in-law holding out his hand to him. With a smile on his face he continued to speak: "Well, now that you are more or less engaged you can have a little bit of fun already. But make sure you keep off the big honey pot, until the pastor has given you his blessing. Do you know what I mean? Or do I have to speak more plainly?"

"No, that is not necessary."

Eduard was glad when his future father-in-law finally let go of his hand. The awkwardness of the situation was written all over his face. He wished he was somewhere else at the mere thought of the word honey pot. Until now, he had never had any difficulties talking about intimate issues – it even used to be fun talking to guys of the same age. But now he had been the centre of discussion, which made him feel completely exposed. And, Karl was an experienced man, knowing all the tricks. He himself would most probably have ignored such instructions when he once wooed Christine. Nothing else could be expected from this Karl Exner.

When Eduard entered the kitchen, everybody stared at him, grinning. Friedrich, Gottlieb, Serafine, Christine, Martha – what they were thinking was written in their faces. Of course, they had listened at the door and thanks to Karl's piercing voice they had heard every single word. Gottlieb wanted to make a coarse remark, but Katlika poked her brother in the ribs with her elbow, and then approached Eduard.

From the parlour Karl's voice rang out: "Well, starting from today onwards, you may kiss her."

"But remember to touch her only as far as the waistline!" shouted Gottlieb.

"Will you shut up!" his mother snapped at him.

"That goes for you too, Katlika," added Gottlieb, while Christine gave him a slap on the back of the head.

"Well, you'll just have to endure such awkwardness, Eduard," said Friedrich to his future brother-in-law, when they were sitting together at Friedrich's house later on.

While Serafine nursed her little daughter in the kitchen, both men had made themselves comfortable in the pleasantly warm living room.

"Since you're getting married after Easter, it won't be too bad if you do not obey everything exactly as father Karl has told you. In reality, the old man doesn't believe you'll keep your hands to yourself. However, since we have winter now, it's a must that you look for a warm little place in order to do certain activities. Otherwise you're in danger of getting a cold bottom."

"Friedrich!" yelled Serafine from the kitchen now, "stop trying to corrupt Eduard. Please think of your sister's innocence."

"My God," said Eduard, "how embarrassing that was. I could just as well have stood on the table, naked... it really felt like everybody was examining me."

"We can still catch up on this," snorted Friedrich, "I know a few women who would take part in it with great interest."

Having finished breastfeeding, Serafine came to the door now and said: "Stop bothering my little cousin. He's been through a lot today!"

"Anyone who wants my sister's honey pot must be able and willing to patiently bear all this."

Now Eduard gave his future brother-in-law a friendly hook to the chin and both men started to laugh until tears came into their eyes.

Serafine shook her head: "Friedrich, I always thought you were the most sensible man in the family, but, when it comes to craziness, you are in no way inferior to your father."

Katlika married Eduard Ehmke shortly after Easter. And Serafine's brother, Rudolf, married Pauline Ehmke, a cousin of Eduard and Serafine. As a funny coincidence, the maiden name of Rudolf's mother was also Pauline Ehmke. Thus, some friends took great delight in saying: “Couldn’t you just take your time to search for another wife? Nothing can be so urgent that one has to marry one’s own mother.” However, the degree of relationship between both Paulines was very distant.

Volhynia 1914

– 11 –

Again, it was summer in Volhynia. It was a hot day in Janowka. The women brought lunch out to the fields to provide for their husbands, children as well as the farm workers. Serafine, Friedrich, her parents-in-law – Christine and Karl – as well as Aljoscha, the Ukrainian farm worker, and his son Michail were sitting in a circle under the shade of a tree spooning up their soup. Serafine had already fed her little daughters earlier on, and then put them to bed for an afternoon nap. Martha was working in the garden today and was supposed to check on them.

Suddenly, Karl's eyes were unable to leave the main road. There was something going on. He got up and said: "Well, what does that mean?"

In the meantime, all the others had risen, too. A cloud of dust. After a while a carriage pulled by four horses could be made out accompanied by four riders both in front of and behind the carriage.

"Those are Russian soldiers," said Friedrich and headed to the road. "I want to know what they want."

Karl accompanied him and in a few minutes they reached the area in front of the parish hall where more than a hundred other villagers were already gathered. And more and more people came flocking. One of the soldiers nailed a sheet in Russian text on the door of the parish hall. Heading: General mobilization. Signatory: Tsar Nicolaus II.

Finally, the uniformed man from the carriage rose, signalled the crowd to be quiet, and spoke loudly in Russian: "His Majesty, Tsar Nicolaus II, declared war on the German Empire on the 30th of July, 1914."

Looks beyond belief, naked fear, cries of horror, women moaning. The man in uniform continued reading. At the word mobilization many of the listeners, again, made sounds of disbelief.

"The following men must appear here at this place tomorrow morning at seven o'clock: Abel Maximilian, Brandt Heinrich....., Exner Friedrich, Exner Gottlieb....... Hinz Wilhelm...... Rattai......"

Of the approximately one hundred and sixty village men, fifty were called upon to enlist in the armed forces within twenty-four hours.

"Those who do not obey this order, will be sentenced to death by hanging!"

The villagers dropped everything. The work in the field rested. Some had gone home or to the neighbours to discuss what to do. But there was no alternative. One had to obey or one was dead. Serafine, her husband and her parents-in-law, Gottlieb and the neighbours, Emil and Caroline Gehrmann, were sitting together behind her house. Emil did not have to join the forces because he wasn't so young any more. For the time being, the army was focused on recruiting men under thirty. Christine sat, like in a trance, on the garden bench. In the last hours, she had shed so many tears that she could not cry any more. Picturing both sons going to war was simply unbearable.

"Now it's up to us, Karl," said Emil Gehrmann. "When the boys are away, we must work twice as much. Thank God, my sons aren't old enough yet. But for my daughter's boyfriend it will get serious now, too. Being a German officer in the Russian army, they will put him at the very front, I suppose. Anyway, we must stick together now. Of course, I will help you bring in the harvest. Especially since we don't know whether they'll leave us the Ukrainian harvesters or whether the Tsar will take them away too."

"Where will our men be sent?" asked Serafine.

"First, they'll be stationed in a camp near Kostopol where they'll be given their medicals. The lucky ones will be sent home again. Those who are healthy, however, will do training. Hopefully, everything will have calmed down by then. I don't think the German emperor is going to send troops against Russia just because the Tsar has declared war on him. And the Austrian will keep still too, as he's up to his neck with the Serbians, the Italians, the Hungarians and the Romanians. This whole nightmare will probably be gone in a few weeks and the 'fine gentlemen' will end up drinking with each other. We shouldn't get ourselves in a crazy state now!"

Serafine heaved a sigh and said: "Please God, I hope you're right. Oh, if we had only listened to Salomon. He told us over and over again: Go, and emigrate to Canada."

"But who wants to leave his homeland?" Karl asked, thoughtfully.

Late that night Christine was still sitting alone in the kitchen. She simply could not sleep. The whole situation was very upsetting to Karl. He, who was always so quick-witted and full of energy, had gone to bed. *I have hardly ever seen him so helpless,* thought Christine. *To him there's more at stake than just the work which must now be done without the boys. He's seriously worried about his sons. He is so proud of them. They're so much like him. Even if Friedrich is a rather thoughtful type, rational and not as loud as Gottlieb and Karl, both boys, nevertheless, are cast in the same mould like their father. They complement each other in such a way that Karl is revealed. It had been a pleasure to see them growing up. Not for anything in the world would I want to miss the tricks they played on their father that would drive him insane. And this has remained so until today. They still engage in a lot of nonsense. Gottlieb even more than Friedrich. That's just the way it is – that's their father's legacy. Karl himself wouldn't want to miss an opportunity to fool around either.* A little smile formed on the edges of Christine's mouth. *And how nicely they have looked after their little sisters. That, too, has remained until today.* Christine drank from the milk she had just poured and took a deep breath. *And now? Now Serafine is alone with her two little girls – and she's expecting another child. It's good we live so close to each other. I can help her, and Martha will be there, too. If only the boys come back safe and sound.* The smile left her face and she shouted loudly: "Damn it! Why must these cursed emperors and kings make war?! They should go and beat themselves up. Why should this concern us?"

It was rare for sensible Christine to vent her anger this way. But to-day was an exceptional day.

The next morning the whole village assembled in front of the parish hall. In addition, there were people from more distant farms as well as from Solomiak. Rudolf, Serafine's brother, as well as Eduard, Katlika's husband, were also targeted. Since both men lived in Solomiak, Serafine had just found out about it this morning – although she'd already had a sense of foreboding yesterday. Until now the Russians, occasionally, had refused to call up some men, in particular if they were needed on a farm. Sometimes money helped persuade the authorities to decide that way. But now it was war!

A Russian soldier read out the names of those who should step forward. Another one checked names off a list. When a name was called, the person concerned had to step forward and line up in a row opposite the villagers. The men carried bundles with their laundry and, above all, plenty of food, because it was known that ordinary soldiers were kept in short supply.

One person who was called was absent – Anton, a farmer the same age as Friedrich. He had a family with five children to support. His wife stepped forward on his behalf explaining that her husband was ill. The captain, who was mounted on his horse, immediately gave a harsh order to get the missing man. Four riders accompanied Anna, Anton's wife, to her house. Anna could hardly keep pace, with the riders who forced her on. After a few minutes they came back. Anton's hands were tied up as he hobbled along behind the horse of a soldier. The villagers were paralysed with horror. Finally, the rider stopped and shooed Anton before the captain. The captain raised his arm as high as he could and cracked his whip on Anton's back. Some people wailed. Then, a soldier roared some instructions and the column started moving. At the head were six riders followed by more than fifty raw recruits on foot, trailed again by some riders with the captain in their middle. Serafine gazed after the column with tears in her eyes, while Christine held Anna in her arms trying to comfort her. But Anna was unable to calm down and refused to accept what was happening to her husband.

"I just don't believe it," she moaned continuously. "Yesterday everything was still all right, and now they're taking our men away. How are we supposed to carry on? Who will get all the work done and how will I ensure my children have enough to eat?"

"Calm down, Anna," said Christine while she softly stroked her hair. "We must stick together. You are not alone."

"I wish I'd taken the whip from that bastard of a captain and cracked it on him for a change," Karl said to Emil Gehrmann, as both sat together in the garden later on that evening.

"The customs in the Russian army are hard," said Emil "and not only in the Russian one. Ordinary soldiers are mistreated everywhere. However, don't you worry too much about your boys; they'll get through it."

"Let's hope so, by goodness! The Tsar has already gotten into fights with so many. A skirmish here, an attack there. But it hasn't affected us personally, so far. Who gives a horseshit if he makes war with the Japs who, by the way, gave him a bloody good hiding. However, we didn't notice much of it, did we? But everything is different now that Germany and Austria are our opponents."

Both men kept on discussing politics, until Christine came and said: "I think, this day was hard enough for all of us. And from tomorrow on we must work twice as much. So, you'd better get to bed."

– 12 –

Utterly exhausted, the men rested on the grounds of a huge encampment east of Kostopol and spooned soup from tin bowls. They hadn't come only from Janowka, but also from several other villages in the area, about five hundred men altogether. Eduard had a hard time. He had kept up the six-hour march only with great difficulty. Anton was doing even worse. He had constantly fallen behind during the march, and each time one of the mounted soldiers had cracked the whip over his back. After two hours he had finally collapsed, and the captain had ordered to put him to be draped over a horse. He was now in one of the barracks, being attended by a doctor.

After the short food break the men had to line up in rows of thirty each, and then two rows at a time were led to a small pond. There, they had to take off their clothes and wash themselves or have a bath. After that they were assigned to the lodgings, thirty men per barrack. Fifteen narrow plank beds on the left side and the right side.

The camp consisted of seventeen such barracks. To the north, there was a manor house in which the commander and the higher ranks resided. Next to it stood a smaller building with further lodgings. The Russian soldiers lived at the other end of the site in hastily assembled timber houses. It appeared that the Germans were still being kept separate from the Russians, as if there were special plans for them. Beside the Russian lodgings there was the kitchen house from where the soldiers were called to pick up their meals which were to be eaten outdoors. At the extreme end, there was another building, probably once a barn, where the weapons and uniforms were kept. Next to that were the horse stables. The latrines were located west of the camp, approximately twenty meters away from the barracks.

Next morning, a shrill almost murderous whistle followed by the roaring of two soldiers made Friedrich jump out of bed; others copied him shortly afterwards. Those not quick enough were either threatened with the whip or actually got a taste of it. In groups of thirty, the men went to the serving hut where everyone had to pick up a bowl of porridge. Then every group was led to the manor house. At the entrance a table was set up where the captain and a scribe sat. In front of the table was a doctor in a white coat – a friendly elderly man, well-fed, chubby-cheeked, with a shiny bald head. A few meters away from the doctor stood a soldier responsible for bringing each man to him individually. The other men, all naked, had to remain lined-up until they were handed over to the doctor. The doctor examined each individually but in a superficial way, putting his stethoscope to the chest, looking into the mouth, examining backbone and feet. Now and then he would ask a man something, dictating a few words to his secretary. Almost all men were finished their medicals in two minutes. Only a few, among them Eduard, had three to four minute medicals.

Those who had passed the examination had to hurry to the other end of the camp to the wardrobe centre. They left there wearing the simple uniforms of Russian soldiers, and then they were entitled to receive soup and bread from the kitchen.

Afterwards they had to queue up for the barbers who had been going about their businesses in the open giving each a short military haircut.

Early in the evening all kitted out soldiers were mustered for roll call. First, the captain, roaring as usual, recited a litany of regulations. Then the commander, a good-natured cheery man in his fifties, spoke, much more quietly and more powerfully than the captain, and the new soldiers listened with rapt attention:

"Soldiers! Russia is at war. We expect the German Empire to attack our beloved fatherland. Normally, all Germans living in this area would be sent far to the east, so that they can neither collaborate nor spy with their attacking compatriots against Russia. However, showing his good will, our beloved Tsar Nicolaus II. has decided to give the Germans a chance. Now's your chance! Obey and be good soldiers. Defend our home country which is also your home country. Whoever takes advantage of the Tsar's good-naturedness and is caught in the act of sabotage or espionage, will be hung with no mercy, and his family will be banned to Siberia..."

How did I get here?, Friedrich asked himself. *What are we doing here anyway? And what's this all about? What for? I don't care about the German emperor, and the Austrian one either. I have a wife and two children, soon there will be three. I have a farm I must be looking after. Instead of working, loving my wife, cuddling my children and playing with them, I'm now supposed to learn how to kill people. You are all crazy!* Unlike his companions who soaked up every single word of the commander, he didn't grasp anything at all because his mind was on something completely different. On Serafine who's expecting their third child. On his daughters, his mother, his father... *How will all the work be done? It's impossible for Serafine to look after all the animals, feed the pigs, milk the cows, check on the horses and the poultry, muck out and and and... No way! And how's she going to bring in the harvest on her own if they also took Aljoscha, our seasonal worker? And since Gottlieb is here with me, he won't be able to help either Serafine or our parents. Everything will probably collapse. And what will I do if it gets serious? Whom should I shoot then? Germans, Austrians? And if I get shot myself? Or come home as a cripple no longer able to work? What's it like to be dead? Do we go on living in another form like Serafine so strongly believes? Or do we just turn into nothing? Why am I standing here? I'd give everything to be at home.*

– 13 –

Late at night there was a loud knocking at Katlika's door. The young woman startled from sleep. Then someone called: "Katlika, open up! It's me."

Could that be Eduard's voice? With a pounding heart she went down the stairs, unbolted and opened the door and... indeed.

"Eduard!"

Exhausted to death he just fell into her arms.

"I'm shattered."

Katlika dragged him onto one of the kitchen chairs, took off his shoes and was horrified at the sight of his feet which were covered in blisters and blood. With effort, she somehow managed to bring him upstairs and put him to bed. He had just enough strength to explain to her that they did not want him in the army on account of poor health.

The following morning he had recovered to the extent that he could tell Katlika the whole story at the breakfast table. During that horrible march he had suffered from severe dfficulties in breathing, and had side stitches over and over, so that Friedrich and Rudolf had to support him. The next morning the doctor had pronounced him not fit. Late in the afternoon he was sent home, together with a few other men from the area who had also been unfit for service. The march back, however, had been so strenuous that, despite being full of happy anticipation of coming home again, they had made headway very slowly.

"At least I am with you again. Anna is much worse off. Anton passed away yesterday afternoon. He really had been ill. Having to march during that dreadful heat was too much for him. When we finally arrived, he was more dead than alive. May God have mercy on his soul."

"... and on his wife and five children who must now grow up without their father" said Katlika with tears in the eyes as she pulled a handkerchief out of her apron.

After a few days Eduard had recovered more or less; so that he was able to work on the farm again as usual. One afternoon, Martha came riding to Solomiak and met up with Eduard in the pigpen.

"Well, sister-in-law, what leads you here at this time of the day? Don't you have anything to do?"

"Father has died. He collapsed in the field. There was nothing we could do for him."

"What? Karl?"

Martha burst into heavy sobbing as she sank into her brother-in-law's arms. Katlika and Martha set off together shortly afterwards to be with their mother and give her support.

The burial was even more dreary than a burial usually is. Both sons, Friedrich and Gottlieb, now soldiers of His Majesty the Tsar, weren't allowed to come. Christine was supported by her daughters. The choir sang: *Jesus Christ, my sure Defense and my Savior, ever liveth; knowing this, my confidence rests upon the hope it giveth.*

The whole village was present as well as the people from the colonies of Janowka and Solomiak. Karl had been only 55 years old, always looking the very picture of health, and as strong as an ox. Nobody had ever reckoned with this. Now Christine was all alone.

Karl was dead and her sons in the war.

Standing at her husband's grave, Christine thought of her sons. *How must they feel now? They knew their father was to be buried today, but they weren't allowed to come. They'll suffer all their lives not having said a proper good-bye,* she thought. *Dying is as normal as life. But it needs a few things to be able to cope with it.* After all those present had offered their condolences, Christine still remained at the grave with her daughters. Nobody spoke a word. All tears had ceased to flow. She pictured her husband hatching some nonsense together with his sons. How dreadfully furious he'd been when the boys had made fun of him for a change. They ran away, laughing, while he threatened them with a stick. And finally, she remembered how he took his daughters on his lap playing hop, hop, rider when they were still very small. Now, an almost inconspicuous little smile played about her mouth. *Oh Karl, how am I supposed to carry on without you? It has been such a marvellous life with you. What will the future have in store for me?*

For the time being, the future looked like this: A few days later Cossacks – infamous Tatar horsemen – rode through the village. Being partially enemies amongst themselves, some in the Tsar's employ, others fighting against him, they, in most people's opinion, were as unpredictable as they were frightening. The horde consisted of about twenty riders who had been ordered to requisition horses, cattle and food for the army. Of course, those in the army knew what effect the presence of the Cossacks would have on ordinary people. Their ruthless conduct brought success. Before the Cossacks came for a visit there were six horses on Christine's summer paddock, after they left there were only two. They also took cows, pigs, poultry and helped themselves in cellar storerooms and vegetable gardens. Christine's experience was similar to the all the others in the village. As well, the armed horde had recruited several Ukrainians to drive the livestock westward and to load the plundered food supplies onto wagons.

In the evening when Christine, Serafine, Martha and Caroline Gehrmann were sitting together behind the house, Serafine said: "They'll come back over and over again, until there's nothing left."

In October, three hundred soldiers entered Janowka. Apart from some Ukrainians, there were probably as many Russians as Germans. Among them there were several men who had come from the area, including Friedrich and Gottlieb. Serafine saw her husband again for the first time since he had been conscripted. He was a fine figure in his dark Russian uniform. In the meantime, Serafine's belly had been growing. The child was to be born at the end of November.
The army had confiscated some houses to accommodate the higher ranks. The ordinary soldiers lived in tents which were put up between the village and the colony of Janowka. The army helped itself to the farmers' meat, milk, eggs, flour, fruit or vegetables. After a while food became scarce. Would there be enough to get through the winter?

After a few months war had already been fought on many fronts. They found out a lot from the weekly which came regularly from Odessa. Although there were some Russian newspapers circulated in the villages, no one trusted them much because everything they printed was considered to be dictated by the Tsar. For a long time, Jewish merchants travelling throughout the villages had always been the best source for news. But hardly anyone came anymore. Even Salomon from Kostopol hadn't come for two weeks now. It was known, however, that the Germans kept sending loads of soldiers to the Western front to fight against France. Units had also been deployed in the east, but, being rather defensive in their orientations, their primary goal had been to resist Russian attacks by every means. However, they didn't succeed. The Russian army attacked East Prussia which, geographically, extended far into the Russian Empire and, thus, had always intensely annoyed the Tsar. On the other hand, the Russians were driven back during the battle of Tannenberg ending in a disaster with 30,000 fallen soldiers and 95,000 prisoners of war. A little later, the Russian army took the offensive against the Kingdom of Galicia which, being under Austro-Hungarian rule, was located further south, in the immediate neighborhood of Volhynia. However, holding the newly-gained territory proved to be rather difficult, because in order to do so more and more soldiers had to be sent even further south. Since the ruling young Turks of the Ottoman Empire had formed an alliance with Austria-Hungary and the Germans, several Russian Black Sea ports were attacked. Even Serbia, traditionally being supported by Russia against the Austrians, was burning.

However, the Austro-Hungarian army in Galicia was not completely defeated by the Russian occupation. Most of the troops pulled back to the Carpathians, but some units also entered Volhynian soil – and that would be Friedrich's undoing.

"If it's a boy, we shall call him Gottfried," said Serafine to Friedrich who had a few hours leave and sat in the kitchen with his wife and both daughters.

"That's a good name," said Friedrich.

"We'll ask Gottfried then if he would like to be the godfather. And you pick someone else from your family."

"Of course. Maybe I'll ask my cousin Gottfried, then the names will also match. Actually, Rudolf and Pauline wanted to name their son Gottfried, too. But our child is probably going to be born a little bit earlier. Then Rudolf can't call his next son Gottfried. But it doesn't matter if there's one Gottfried more or less."

Friedrich had to laugh: "Gottlieb, Gottfried, Friedrich, all these names express God's love and peace – in the middle of war!" His laughter turned into thoughtfulness. "Well, have you still got enough to eat?"

"I don't know how we will make it through winter," answered Serafine. "Hopefully they'll allow us to keep the last cow, so that the children at least have milk."

"It's bad," said Friedrich. "When I think of how good we've had it throughout the years. Well, the army is also hungry. Most of what they've been taking from the farmers here goes directly to East Prussia which has been marked by the ravages of war. There's nothing left to take from the farmers over there since they were driven back by the Germans."

"What is one supposed to make of that? How is it possible to plunge flourishing countries into wastelands of misery within such a short time? I believe our leaders, in their entirety, are ungodly people," answered Serafine. "They just disregard the Commandments, they kill, steal and lie."

"Maybe! But there's one thing I know for sure... my wife would have made a good pastor," said Friedrich smiling.

Serafine had not only been religious, but also well versed in the Bible. Moreover, she used the Commandments in everyday life, quoting from the Holy Bible and philosophizing. The pastor once told her she had all the makings to take his place.

– 14 –

It was a cold November day when the Austrian captain resolved not to move southwards with his company in order to seek shelter from Russian troops in the Carpathian Mountains. That was not an option anymore since the Tsarist army had already blocked their path. In expectation of German attacks, Galicia as well as the Western border of Volhynia was crowded with Russians. The only chance now was to move northwards and remain east of Kostopol until the Germans broke through the border or the Austro-Hungarian army would overrun the Russian positions from the south. Furthermore, it was some kind of comfort to know that they had not been the only scattered company; other units had also retreated from their southern positions, because they had no other choice. Basically, they were enclosed in enemy territory. However, the strange thing was that they would hardly encounter considerable resistance from the Russian army which, in case of having to react to any expected German offensive, had been bound in the west as well as in the south. Even when they had still been struggling to recover from heavy losses at the battles of Tannenberg and the Masurian lakes, the Russians, undoubtedly, would spare no effort to defend the newly-gained territory in the southwest. Moreover, the Turks had been attacking from the southeast both from the Black Sea and ashore. However, being stuck in the Ukraine surrounded by Russians had been far from relaxing, but there was no way out at the moment. Anyway, with a little luck one would survive the situation, knowing that support was *bound to arrive* sooner or later.

Early in the morning Serafine was woken up by the sound of horses clip-clopping on the road in front of her house. She laboriously crawled out of bed which, in view of her big belly, was not an easy task. When she looked out of the window, she saw at least a hundred soldiers in Russian uniforms riding past at a gallop. The riders turned off at the field opposite of Christine's house a little further down the road. She believed to have recognised her husband among the soldiers as well as his uncle who was also called Friedrich. What was going on there? All of a sudden shots could be heard followed by rumbling cannon fire. Then she noticed her small girls pulling her by the nightshirt crying. *For God's sake – the children!* She pulled her daughters away from the window, hurried down the stairs with them as fast as possible into the cellar. Even there one still heard the shells of the howitzers.

A few houses further away, Katlika, who since her father's death had often been at her mother's place, stood at the window observing what was going on. One shell hit the field causing several Russian soldiers and their horses to fall. Then some deafening rattling began. That had to be one of those dreadful new guns which was able to fire more than a hundred rounds per minute. There! That was Friedrich riding further to the front until his horse fell. He tumbled off and rolled. He didn't move anymore. Then – all of a sudden – it was silent. The Russian soldiers headed back towards the road. *For Heaven's sake! Hurry to Friedrich's aid! Get him off the field!*

"There's Friedrich. He's lying there and doesn't move," it came blurting out of Katlika as if the soldiers could hear her. About fifty yards away from her house, Friedrich's uncle, the brother of Karl, moved towards a horse. The captain roared at him gesticulating to pull back. But, without wavering, he mounted his horse and rode out to his nephew while his superior continued to roar and gesticulate. When he reached Friedrich, he jumped off the horse, looked at him briefly, heaved him up on the back of the horse, remounted and finally rode back. When he reached the captain, he got hit in the face.

In the meantime, Christine and Martha joined Katlika who, in a matter of seconds, had told them everything, shouting: "There's Friedrich! The one they're getting off the horse, that's Friedrich!"

The three women got dressed in next to no time and rushed out of the door. Someone had already laid Friedrich on a wagon and rode towards the other end of the village to the soldier's camp. Christine told Martha to go and get Serafine and remain at her house to look after the children. A few minutes later Christine, Katlika and Serafine arrived at the soldier's camp. Knowing the women, the guard let them pass on to the medical tent. They had to stop at the entrance, as the doctor was just looking after Friedrich. After covering up the patient the doctor came to the women with a serious expression on his face.

"I am so sorry, ladies, but there's nothing more I can do. These are too many bullet wounds. An operation would be pointless. Say goodbye to him; he's still conscious."

I guess I'm dying now, thought Friedrich. *Funny, I never imagined it would be like this. It doesn't hurt at all. I'm bleeding and I can hardly breathe, but there's no pain. What's worse is that I'm starving. If only I had something to eat. There comes Serafine... and Mother... and Katlika is here, too. I'm so glad my women are here by my side. Only Martha is now missing. Please don't cry. Everything will be all right. I'm fine, and soon I'll even be better when Father picks me up. I'm sure we'll have as much fun as in the past. I'm looking forward to it.*

The three women crouched down at Friedrich's plank bed which was separated from the others by a draped sheet. Friedrich was deathly pale. Christine stroked his black hair while his wife took his hand.

"I'm so hungry," said Friedrich.

Hungry? How on earth can one be hungry in the face of death? However, Katlika hurried to an orderly asking him for something to eat. Being surprised and not knowing what to do at such short notice – he had no access to the food panty – he, nevertheless, quickly ran away and came back a few seconds later holding a spoon of sugar. With tears in her eyes, Serafine held the spoon to Friedrich's mouth and he uttered a long 'mmmm', a sound of pleasure, and died.

Serafine was unable to realize what had just happened. Still being a young woman herself, having two little children and soon about to give birth to another one, she was already a widow. Friedrich was twenty-nine years old. Their unborn child would never get to know its father. Christine, Serafine and Katlika walked back home arm in arm with each other. Tears kept running down their faces. The villagers they came across dared not speak to them while they were in that condition and only gazed at them with bewilderment. When they reached Serafine's house, they fetched Martha and the children and everybody went over to Christine's. While sitting at the kitchen table, they gave into their grief. Little by little, relatives and neighbours came over to sympathize with the women in their suffering. Some made themselves useful, looking after the small girls or preparing the meals they had brought.

Late in the afternoon Christine finally made up her mind:

"Serafine, you and the children are moving in with me. You can't be alone anymore in your condition. Besides, nobody knows what else is in store for us. Martha, will you please go and get a room ready for Serafine upstairs; the children will sleep in my room."

Several friends and relatives went over to Serafine's place to get the most essential things. Emil led the cow to Christine's stable, another one caught the remaining chickens.

Christine lay in bed with her two granddaughters who nestled up against her. *I could go on crying forever. And I feel like screaming. But I can't! These little girls need me. What kind of grandmother would*

I be for them if I just lost control of myself? Serafine needs me, too. The baby is due very soon. There isn't any time for moaning and crying.

Serafine lay in the neighbouring room picturing the last minutes she had shared with Friedrich over and over again. His hunger, the spoonful of sugar, the long 'mmmm' – then he'd passed away. Despite his severe injuries it appeared as if he was smiling. *I'll carry this picture with me to the end of my days,* she thought. *But how am I supposed to carry on without him? First, there is this new life coming into the world and both girls need me. Dear God, please give me the strength to make it through all of that.*

Katlika, too, could not sleep. She was lying in bed with Martha.

"Martha, are you sleeping yet?"

"No, how can I sleep after all that has happened today? I can't stop thinking of Friedrich. I couldn't say good-bye to him, and I'll never see him again."

Then she began to cry, and Katlika stroked her head. When, after a while, Martha had managed to fall asleep, Katlika got up and crept into her mother's room. In the darkness, she saw the outlines of both small girls sleeping peacefully in Christine's arms. She quietly closed the door and entered Serafine's room.

"Are you asleep?" she whispered.

"No," answered Serafine softly. "But you don't need to be worried about me. I'm doing fine. But it's good you're here."

The village was marked by a hectic rush during the next few days. Other Russian units were deployed to Janowka to form a starting point to chase after Austrian companies whose path to the south was blocked. Serafine's unoccupied house was immediately confiscated, and with the forceful seizure of livestock and food, the farmers were bleeding again.

A delegation of the Russian army appeared at the burial. A captain put his arms around Serafine and Christine to express his sympathy. The whole village was present on the small cemetery singing *O take my hand, dear Father, and lead Thou me, till at my journey's ending*

I dwell with Thee. Absent, however, was Friedrich, the uncle and namesake of the dead. He had been put in detention because he had disobeyed his captain's order by trying to get his nephew out of the line of fire.

When everything was over, Christine said: "Well, he has gone home now to be with his father Karl as well as with his Heavenly Father. And now it's about time we take care of the living."

She was absolutely right about that. In the evening Serafine went into labour; and early next morning Gottfried saw the light of day which was anything but friendly those days. The situation would become even more unfriendly.

– 15 –

At the beginning of December, the new arrival was baptized by the sexton in Christine's parlour. While Serafine was delighted about her healthy son, she was deeply saddened by the loss of her beloved husband. The Christmas that followed was the saddest ever. Friedrich and Karl were dead. Moreover, Gottlieb as well as her brother Rudolf, like most men from the area, were transferred to another unit. They were probably sent in the direction of Turkey so that they wouldn't be able to meet any attacking Germans. Instead, more and more soldiers from the interior of the Russian Empire came to Janowka. They all needed provisions. Hence, the situation in the village became more and more desperate.

On January 25, Pastor Mueller from Tuczyn came to Janowka to deliver Gottfried's baptism certificate to Serafine and, of course, to express his condolences to the family.

"The times are bad," said the pastor when he had joined Christine and Serafine at the kitchen table. "And from what I've been hearing on my travels it's not getting any better in the near future. They say the Germans aren't far from here. That means there will be heavy battles in our area, Germans will shoot Germans. The world has gone insane. The Russians are afraid of us changing sides. It is rumoured that they want to get rid of us and take us out of here – eastwards... to Siberia."

"But that's impossible!" Christine said energetically. "We've accepted Russian citizenship of our own free will, because we live in this country and consider it our homeland. We have never done any harm to a Russian. My son died for Russia, shot by Austrian soldiers, despite the fact that my late husband's ancestors had themselves been Austrians. My daughter-in-law is now widowed, and must care for three little children. They just can't take away our home, our farms and all that we've worked so hard for."

"I'm afraid they can, dear Christine. War reveals the evil in man. I've never seen as much ungodliness as in these times," replied the pastor putting his hand on Christine's.

"Now, there's nothing we can do but pray, dear women."

Volhynia 1915

– 16 –

Things came to pass as the pastor had predicted. Throughout the spring there was hardly any livestock left in the village. The army took almost everything. Furthermore, groups of soldiers, always hungry, would help themselves to whatever they wanted without their superior's permission. There was no more milk for the children. People prepared their fields and vegetable gardens in the hope of bringing in a rich harvest. Sometimes, before the first light of day, women of the village would sneak to the soldiers' camps hoping to grab some entrails and meat scraps such as tripes, cow heads and the like which, because of the sheer excess of a good meal, would be just thrown away. Sometimes these scraps were already decomposing. The women took everything along in order to make a soup consisting of water, bones and whatever they had managed to grab. As a result, more and more people were dying of food poisoning, so that the little cemetery gradually reached the brink of its capacity.

"What have you brought back from tonight's raid?" asked Serafine while she nursed her son. The two little girls romped cheerfully about on the floor.

"A cow's tail," replied Martha.

"Do you reckon it's still edible?"

"Yes, it smells alright."

Martha was busy at the stove. Then she put two cups of tea on the table and joined Serafine.

"It's good that you still have enough milk. There are, for the time being, no cows left in the village."

"True. But I need to eat something in order to keep on producing milk for awhile."

"I've added some honey to your camomile tea. Thank God they haven't found it. But I have a very special hiding place. In the cellar there's a wall with a loose stone. I hollowed out some space behind it. Nobody will ever find that!"

"It's just crazy one has to hide a bit of honey as if it was some treasure."

"It *is* our treasure. To be honest, it's the last bit of food left in the house. Herbal tea might be healthy, but I doubt anyone can live on it."

"We're going to have vegetables again soon," replied Serafine.

"I'm looking forward to finally having beans again. Right now, I could kill for some bean soup."

"Martha, please say you're only kidding."

"Well, since nobody in Janowka has any bean soup, you don't need to be afraid of your sister-in-law becoming a murderer."

"I prefer that you're just a cow tail thief."

"Who do you call a thief? Who's robbing whom?"

"I know", said Serafine. "Wherever hunger rules, there's theft and robbery. I truly believe God would forgive me if I stole for my children's sake. But I'd never kill."

"Oh, Serafine," answered Martha while she caressed Gottfried's bare feet, "I think in certain situations I wouldn't stop myself from killing someone. I am sometimes so angry that I could just start blindly hitting. And if someone did something to the little ones, I would strangle him, believe me."

"Listening to you talk, I believe you."

"I am unfortunately not like the Mennonites," said Martha and lay her hands on the table. "They'd rather die than defend themsel-ves."

Serafine finished breastfeeding and laid her little son into Martha's arms. While she buttoned up her blouse, she said: "I think we've had enough murderous thoughts for today. In fact, we haven't done anyone harm, whether it's been friend or foe. And that's how it should remain."

In July, the food situation became more stable. The emaciated people had fresh vegetables in their gardens again. Meanwhile, the army had become more disciplined in its food distribution, so that there was something for everyone. And the grain! My goodness! thought Serafine, the grain has never looked better. One could count on a prosperous harvest. But it got worse after all...

Ogema, Saskatchewan Canada 1931

– 17 –

"Mum, the letter from Regina has arrived! A big envelope!" shouted Rudolf junior as he rushed into the kitchen.

"Well, we already know what's written in there," replied his mother.

"Sure, but it's a good feeling to know that we're finally Canadians. What are we having for lunch, by the way?"

"Russian borscht for German Canadians who've come from the Ukraine."

"Awesome!" answered Rudolf as he opened the big envelope. "There are four certificates. And there we've got it in black and white: Rudolf, Rudolf junior, Pauline and Gottfried Rattai. Now we're all Canadians. By the way, there's another letter – from Germany. It's from Aunt Serafine. Here it is."

"And you just mention that in passing? Give it to me!"

The Rattais had come to Saskatchewan where they first had stayed with friends from their old homeland until they had finished building their own place. An uncle of Rudolf who had been living in the west, in British Columbia, occasionally sent some money, so that they were able to tide themselves over the first year and make some essential purchases. Uncle Gottfried had come to Canada before the war and had built his own farm. His profound Christian charity as well as a strong sense to help others, especially relatives and friends, proved to be a real blessing for the new immigrants. After only a few years the Rattais viewed their own vast corn fields. The prairie, without a doubt, had its rough sides. Icy winters, hot dry summers with a shortage of water, long distances to go shopping. But all that was nothing compared to what one had received. Freedom, a self-determined life and the certainty not to be exiled from one's home.

In the evening the family of four sat together in the living room. It was November and there wasn't much left to do outside. One still had to look after the animals and there were repairs to do that had been put off during the busy summer months. Now, everything could be done in comfort and without haste. And if it got too boring, one could cut timber in the nearby woods for one's own requirements or sell it. They were doing well. Rudolf and Pauline had built themselves a little farm. Every year they cleared more acres and since Rudolf Junior was now a young man and a good farmer, they could manage all the work involved. Fourteen-year-old Gottfried contributed his share after school even if farming didn't seem to be his cup of tea. Rudolf glanced up from his sister's letter and studied the enclosed photo a little closer.

"It seems things have gone well for them in Germany. Nevertheless, it'd be better if they were here. I don't trust the peace in Europe. Here we are free. There's plenty of land and those who work hard get rewarded."

"I agree. It was the right decision to come to Canada," replied Pauline.

"When I think back to all the misery I've seen and what we went through in 1915 – that's enough for a whole life."

Volhynia 1915

– 18 –

Early in the morning, on the 9th of July 1915, horsemen came to the village. Cossacks! That was ominous! Serafine and Christine had just finished dressing and feeding the children since they wanted to go into the field to cut the grain. But what happened next would forever be engraved in their memories. The Cossacks pounded on every door and ordered the villagers to pack. In two hours everybody was to be ready to go. The Tsar had ordered all Germans living in Volhynia to flee. In this case, the flight's destination was predetermined: Siberia. Whoever did not follow the request, would be hung.

Serafine yelled at a young Cossack: "It was promised me that I wouldn't have to leave because my husband was killed in this war, my brother's in the army too, and I have three little children. I have a Russian passport as well; so, off with you! Leave us alone!"

"Woman, you're making me laugh. Nobody gives a damn who your husband was, what your brother does or whether you have children. Go pack your stuff, or your children will have no mother!"

Within two hours all the villagers had gathered on the road. Those who still had horses or oxen, harnessed them and stowed onto the wagons everything useful that could be grabbed in a hurry: blankets, clothes, dishes and anything that was left to eat in the house. In the meantime, the people from the colony of Janowka and from Solomiak arrived at the other end of the village. Those who had no more draught animals stacked their belongings onto the wagons of their neighbours. Of course, the villagers wanted to take along as much as possible, but there wasn't enough room. A Cossack climbed up onto an overloaded wagon and began arbitrarily throwing things to the ground. A woman screamed and an old man threatened with his fist. But the Cossack was unperturbed.

Another villager loaded a cage with chickens onto his wagon and was ordered to release them. When the villager refused, the Cossack threw the cage down while the chickens protested and their feathers flew all over the place. Then he pulled out his gun and shot at the cage. The owner of the chickens, an elderly man, went for the Cossack trying to hit the gun out of his hand. But the Cossack turned the weapon on him: "Be careful, old man, or the next bullet will be yours."

A woman rushed in to pull the chicken owner away. Then she turned to the Cossack and said: "God will punish you. He'll punish you all for all you've done to us."

"What should we do now?" Martha asked her mother in desperation.

"We can't do anything," said Christine as she mounted the wagon. "Pass me the kids."

A helpless anger had spread through Christine. This anger stopped her fear from showing. *You damn criminals won't get us down,* she thought.

Then the column started moving. Two Cossacks rode ahead. Crossing the river through a ford near the village was painstakingly slow. The ferry couldn't operate because of the low water level; and besides, it would have taken even longer to move all the wagons. Serafine made her children comfortable on their wagon which was pulled by two horses. She sat up front beside her mother-in-law who led the team. Martha went alongside on foot. People cried and moaned. Having reached the opposite river bank, Christine turned around one last time. When she looked at the ripe grain fields tears came into her eyes. Would she see all that again one day?

I just don't believe it, thought Serafine. *How could this happen? What else is still going to happen?* Then, she was thinking of practical things: *In our haste, have I brought everything we need? Where are my parents? And where is Rudolf's family? They're probably together with Katlika and Eduard at the end of this long caravan. That's how it must be.*

Martha walked beside the carriage in a daze. While others had put on their finest gear, she still wore her work apron. *Protect us, God,* she said to herself. *Protect my little darlings on the wagon. And don't let me die yet, please. I've never had a man so far. Let me experience this before I die.* After a while she became aware of what she was thinking: *Am I just crazy? How can I even think of dying? Rubbish! We're just making a journey. Maybe everything will turn out better than we think at the moment. Dear God, please let us have a good journey. And please let those damn Cossacks' balls wither and fall off. Oh, I'm sorry. I didn't want to think that. It just came to my mind.*

"Martha!"

The girl winced with fright as Serafine had torn her from her thoughts. "Martha, come up, we'll swap places. Sit down for a while and I'll walk for a bit."

"Doesn't Gottfried first have to be nursed?"

"I've just finished. Didn't you notice?"

"No, I was lost in thought."

In the afternoon the column met up with another even bigger group of wagons and joined it. Thus, in a few days, an almost endless caravan was formed. They passed through deserted villages in which only a handful of Poles and Ukrainians were seen standing at the side of the road gazing in bewilderment, not understanding what they were seeing. In the evenings, camps were set up on fields and meadows. Certain families would always group together to cook their meagre supplies. Some were already running out of food. But there were always others who'd share some bits and pieces of their own sparse meals. Along the way, some of the Cossacks constantly tried to scrounge up something edible. They had a carefully guarded wagon filled with provisions which was not just for their own use. Obviously, they had been ordered not to let people starve on the way. However, maybe there were also humanitarian reasons, because they themselves also had mothers, wives and children. In some Ukrainian villages there was not enough water for all the people and animals. The capacity of the shallow Ukrainian wells was not sufficient. So, they were dependent on brooks and rivers which sometimes made some people sick.

One warm summer evening, in the middle of July, Christine, Serafine, Martha, Mathilde and Eduard as well as the Gehrmann family sat together in a circle, in a camp set up in a field near a small lake.

"Where are they taking us?" asked Christine the circle.

"First, we head for Kiev," answered Emil Gehrmann. "There we must leave our horses behind because then we continue by train."

"But where to then? Kiev is already so far."

"In this huge country, Kiev is part of our neighbourhood. One of the Cossacks, a nice guy actually, told me they have orders to escort us to Kiev. There, people will be divided since there are several other groups like us on the way. There must be hundreds of thousands of people whom they want to rid of. Some will be sent directly to the north, others will be sent further eastwards."

"For Heaven's sake – what are we supposed to do there and how will we survive?"

"I think we're being taken to where a lot of work is waiting for us. The kind of work no one else wants to do. There's a lack of manpower because many men have been serving in the army. In fact, almost all the healthy Russian men are now at war. Therefore, we're more than useful to them. And if we're supposed to work, we're going to have to eat. It's probably not going to be as bad as it might seem now. What we need now is hope and trust in God. Without that nothing will work."

It became very quiet after Emil's words of hope and then Serafine started singing the song of Stenka Rasin, a traditional Cossack folk tune she'd always loved. It started out soft, until others joined in and, the song spread gradually throughout the whole camp. The Cossacks also joined in, some however wondering why these particular Germans would sing a song about their icon, Stenka Rasin.

The next day Wilhelmine Ehmke, a fifteen-year-old cousin of Serafine, joined them. She had been walking with Martha beside the carriage, when Serafine said: "Martha, Wilhelmine, come and sit up here for a while and look after the children. I must get some water. It is so hot and we've almost used up our reserves."

Serafine left the boxseat while the wagon was in motion. After both girls had climbed up, Martha took her place beside Christine and Wilhelmine joined the children in the back. While little Gottfried was sleeping, Wilhelmine and Serafine's daughters sang nursery rhymes. After some time she took her songbook and a pencil out of her pocket and began to write.

"What are you writing in there, Wilhelmine?" Christine wanted to know.

"I'm making a note of the places we're passing. When we are back, I'll know all the places where I've been."

"That's a good idea," said Christine.

"I doubt anyone will remember all the places we've passed through. Who knows where else we're still going. I'll just be happy when this trip is over. This is more strenuous than working all day in the field. Oh God, what will happen to our fields? What will happen to our rich harvest?"

"Others will get it," said Martha. "We sow, and the others harvest and eat as much as they want."

After a while Christine said: "Where's Serafine got to? She's been away for quite a while now. That brook should have been only a hundred meters from the road. I hope nothing has happened to her. I think I'll pull over to the side of the road and wait, otherwise she won't catch up with us."

Serafine had lost her bearings. After she'd scooped up water from the brook she'd returned to the column. But where was her wagon? She ran past many teams of horses which were moving forward at a snail's pace. However, she didn't find the carriage led by Christine and Martha. In my haste, I've probably gone past it already. So she ran back. Still, there was no trace of the wagon. In despair, Serafine started to cry. After a while, someone helped her onto a wagon and encouraged her.

"You will soon find your people again," a middle-aged woman said to her. "These bloody Cossacks will make sure that nobody gets lost."

After some time she finally saw the carriage at the side of the road with Christine, Martha, Wilhelmine and the three small children.

"Thank God! I thought I'd never find you again."

It had been a terrible day for Serafine. It was not until the evening, when she held her son in her arms again and the heat had abated, that she was able to let go of all the stress.

"How long will things go on like this?" she asked Christine.

"On one wagon that I passed, a child was being born. On another wagon, a child had just died. All at once, I became so terrified and panic-stricken, I only wanted to see my children. And then, I couldn't find you."

"But you did find us in the end. Everything will be all right," answered Christine.

Just then a Cossack came up to Serafine. It was Sergei, the young man whom she yelled at when they were setting off. Startled, both women wanted to rise from their seats.

"Remain seated, women. I only wanted to bring you something." He passed Serafine a bottle. "Here is some milk for the little child."

"Thank you," said Serafine surprised.

"You've had a bad day, worried about your children. I've watched you, however, I couldn't help you because there's constantly something going on. Wagons break down and I have to fix them. Then I'm sent to find something to eat which has become more and more difficult. And the people always think everything is our fault. But we only do as we are told. This is not our war and we didn't decide to send you away either."

Yes, Serafine thought, *you are people just like us and you only do as you are told. Who makes up all this crap then? Expelling people from their homeland, making war, shooting people. It's a crying shame. But who dares to tell this to the high and mighty?* Serafine was grateful for the breath of humanity released from the young Cossack. Maybe there was a mother or a fiancée worried about him, hoping he would return home again safe and sound. At the moment, there was nothing else that a helpless and insignificant human could do, but to submit to one's fate, and to hope and pray.

Kiev 1915

– 19 –

"My God," said Christine to Serafine. "I have never seen such a big city in my entire life. Just look at those big houses. I wonder who's living there. And the church over there with those crazy towers!"

After many days of hardship, during which the trek made only lethargically slow progress, the long line of wagons finally arrived in Kiev. It was an awful mess in front of the railway station. Street vendors offered their goods to the new arrivals, others wanted to buy their wagons and animals from them. While Christine was engaged in serious negotiations with a cattle dealer, talking to him with a mixture of German, Russian and Yiddish, Wilhelmine came by, completely excited.

"We're going to Orenburg," she said.

"Whereabouts is Orenburg?" Martha wanted to know.

"At the Ural river."

"Oh my goodness," said Martha. "That must be at the end of the world."

At that time Martha could not anticipate yet that her own voyage would lead her much farther away. And she also couldn't know that she'd never see Wilhelmine again.

After everything one couldn't take along was sold, people whose trains weren't ready yet, searched for a little place on the ground where they could rest and wait, either in, or in front of, the station. Quite a few had waited for days. Some wagons had been separated before Kiev was reached, because their destination was still unknown. Those people had to remain at the quite primitive camps, some even for months. Some people were to be sent to the area around Orenburg, others to Ufa or Alma-Ata. All were heading towards the east or to the north. What all people had in common was that nobody knew what to expect. Christine only knew that she, along with her daughters and grandchildren, were heading towards Nowonikolajewsk. It was in the far north. From there, it was farther still. She'd heard that there would be enough work in the factories to earn their living. Thank God they had been accompanied by the Gehrmann family and several others from the village, so that they could support each other.

Who would have thought I'd ever in my life come to Kiev, thought Martha. *One just needs the opportunity to look at everything. And money, to go into the big shops and buy something. I don't think Mother will give me some so I can set off on my own.*

"Martha, come with me, we're going downtown to buy some supplies."

"Oh, how wonderful!"

"Well, I'm not sure if it'll be that wonderful. The prices here are so high that we must calculate exactly what we're spending the money on."

The both set off to spend some of the money Christine had gotten for the horses and the wagon. Of course, Christine was proceeding as economically as possible, predominantly buying preservable food. It goes without saying that she haggled over the price to the last kopeck. The most exciting part for Martha was standing in front of the windows of the luxurious shops. Being a sensible girl, she knew, of course, she could never buy anything for herself. But having the chance to see all that for once in her life was a real experience. With heavy loads, the two returned to the station.

– 20 –

While they waited in Kiev, the group from Janowka met Robert Exner who had run a cloth factory in the southwest, in Berestetschko bordering Galicia. Robert was a brother of Karl. Their father, Karl senior, who had once come from Galicia, had nourished the family from humble beginnings with only one loom at his disposal. His son Robert managed to make the business succeed. Robert married the teacher's daughter, Maria Hahn, whose family had also moved from Galicia to Volhynia. Unfortunately, she had already passed away when the youngest of seven children was only three years old. Robert had not come to the burial of his brother Karl because the news of his death had reached him too late. And when Friedrich died, the chaos of war was already too intense to allow travel.

They also met Augustine, the oldest sister of Serafine, and her two daughters. Finally, Christian Hilscher and his family also appeared. Christian was Christine's brother who had lived in Kopan. Some had not seen each other for many years. Of all places, here at the train station quarter of this big foreign city, while fleeing from Germans and Austrians, everybody got together again.

Robert said that four of his sons had immigrated to Canada before the war broke out. His youngest son, Rudolf, had only been thirteen years old at the time, but his older brothers were looking after him. From their letters one could gather that everybody was well. Two lived in Winnipeg earning their living as craftsmen and window-cleaners. The other two were working on a prairie farm. Their common goal was to save enough money to buy their own farm.

There were constant arguments during the long wait. For example, some people claimed that women whose husbands had been serving in the Russian army ought not to be sent away at all. That, at least, had been the Tsar's decision. However, many local commanders couldn't care less. They just shipped everyone away. One woman, who was affected by this, approached an officer. As he turned his back on her, she pulled him by the uniform making a desperate attempt to ask for a hearing. She became more upset and started to yell. This became too much for the officer, and he pulled out his gun and shot it in the air; then he turned the weapon on the woman and insisted: "Don't you touch me again, woman. The next bullet's going to hit you exactly between your eyes."

If the woman had not left him alone at that very moment, throwing herself to the ground, she would most certainly have been dead. The crying children gathering around her seemed to get on the officer's nerves as well.

"My God, how on earth can a man be that appalling!" yelled Serafine as the officer walked away, while Christine became stiff with panic as her daughter-in-law tangled with such a brutal person.

The next morning everybody got on the train. There were only a few cars with benches, and those were reserved for the guards. Christine, Martha, Katlika and Eduard, Serafine with her three children, as well as the Gehrmanns with their big crowd of children, Serafine's parents and sisters, and Rudolf Rattai, Mrs. Pauline with her small son, together with some other people had been sharing one wagon together. Since the floor was covered with straw, it obviously was meant for carrying cargo or cattle. There were no windows, so that the door had to remain open to prevent suffocation. In the corner was a bucket to relieve oneself. Robert and Christian along with their families had ended up in another train car. Then, the train started slowly moving – towards an uncertain future.

What does our future look like, Serafine asked herself. *Must I raise my children in the high North, far away from home? How will we make a living? Where will we live? Will there be any schools and churches? How are things going now at home? Who's harvesting our fields and who's living in our houses? There are so many questions and not knowing what's going on really wears one down. It probably makes no sense trying to rack one's brain all the time. Man proposes, God disposes. If this is what's been destined for us, we can't escape from it anyway. Maybe God will hold out His helping hands and lead us out of this misery.* Having her Bible handy, as usual, Serafine opened the passage in which God leads His chosen people out of Egyptian slavery into the Promised Land. *Yes,* thought Serafine, *this is what I mean. One must never give up hope. Trust in God. We must simply put our destiny in His hands, for only He gives us security in these times. We can struggle as much as possible, but we won't succeed in getting out of this mire. On the contrary, we're sinking deeper into it. There's only one way out. God will pull us out! This is our only chance.* Being strengthened in her faith, Serafine put aside the Bible and said to her fellow-passengers: "Let's all pray together. It's been a while since we last attended a service. We must not give up our faith now – whatever may come. We have not left God at home. He's been travelling with us. And in these bad times we need Him more than ever."

Though some people were a bit suprised by what the young woman was suggesting, Serafine received a lot of approval. From that moment on, prayers were said together once a day. Afterwards people would sing a hymn.

What a clever daughter-in-law I have, thought Christine. *She herself has a hard time, being without a husband and having to care for three little children on her own. But, still, she manages to give hope to others.*

Russia 1915-1917

– 21 –

The train moved ahead agonizingly slow. Over and over again it stopped between stations, because military transports and freight trains were given priority. Apparently, the human goods transported weren't considered that important. After several unbearably hot days during which people believed they were travelling in an oven rather than on a train, they finally reached the south Russian city of Rostov-on-Don. The passengers were told that the train would stop here for a few hours. Whoever intended to leave the train to make purchases was asked to be back by noon at the latest. Anyone attempting to escape would be shot dead.

Christine and Martha as well as some other women set off to buy some food in town. Her brother, Christian Hilscher from the neighbouring freight car, joined them along with his whole family. Meanwhile, those remaining at the station cleaned the train cars and procured fresh water. Being on the train for such a long time, living in a confined space with so many people, drastically impaired hygiene. The air reeked of diapers and dirty human bodies. After the women had finished cleaning the wagons and had given their children a cold wash on the platform, Serafine kindled a fire on the edge of the railroad area to wash diapers in a big pot. A few other women with toddlers joined her when, all of a sudden, a uniformed railway official appeared, a shrivelled little old man whom one couldn't take very seriously. When he started to yell at the women to immediately extinguish the fire, Serafine collared him.

"You stupid uniformed Grandfather Frost! Would you like to keep travelling through the whole of Russia if you shit your pants? Go away and let us do our job or I'm going to throw a diaper at you!"

"How dare you, you shameless bitch!"

"I could also stuff a diaper in your mouth, a full one, to be precise!"

The other women snorted with laughter and offered diapers to the official. The poor little man's head turned as red as a beetroot and he could do nothing but to threaten with his fist.

"Little old man," Serafine now said in a rather conciliatory tone, "let us do our job – and you go and have a vodka. That's far better than tangling with women who'd do everything for their children, even stuffing shit into the mouths of men in uniform."

The man, whom Serafine in the meantime felt sorry for, couldn't say another word. Looking like he would burst any moment, the man turned around and disappeared, making hasty strides towards the railway station.

Around midday people came back with their purchases. Christine and Martha were heavily loaded, but complained of the prices which were shooting up in the face of war. At home they hadn't been used to buying food. Whether it was meat, vegetables, fruit, milk or bread, they had produced everything themselves. In this foreign city, however, one had to be glad to buy anything at all even at the excessive prices.

"Where has Christian got to?" asked Christine herself. "We're leaving soon."

Another hour passed. Christian and his family did not appear. Christine became more worried. She ran to the railway station entrance, looking out for them. But still, there was no sign of her brother and his family. She went back to the train hoping he'd got there in the meantime. Nothing. *Good God! This is beginning to seriously worry me. We lost sight of each other in town. However, I doubt they got lost. Everybody knows where the railway station is. What happens if the train sets off? Then we're separated, and Christian is stuck with his family in this foreign city not knowing anybody. How will the guards react if somebody's missing? In the end they might get hunted down and shot.*

She had barely expressed her thoughts when a railway official yelled: "Everybody on board! The train's about to leave."

"Good heavens!" shouted Christine.

"You can't leave yet, there are still some people missing."

A soldier standing next to Christine's train car only said: "Those idiots have only themselves to blame. We're setting off now. If they're trying to make a run for it and get caught, they'll simply be shot."

The train started moving while Christine's eyes longed for her brother to appear. But he did not come. Neither him, his wife or the children. Slowly, the train rolled out of the station, out of the town, gathering more and more speed, until only fields and pastures were seen; and after the fields and pastures, there was forest. The watching, the worrying, and dashed hope, had exhausted Christine. Finally, she left the door, collapsed, and gave up hope. She had lost her brother somewhere in the infinite stretches of Russia. She would never see him again.

The train moved day and night, further and further and further. It now headed straight north. It stopped only for coal and water. Sometimes, however, it would stop in the middle of nowhere for no apparent reason. Then, people had the chance to stretch their legs for a bit. Sometimes, they'd be lucky and the train would stop for several hours, which people took as a welcome opportunity to cook outdoors. Since cooking wasn't possible on the train, one could only hope to have enough bread and fruit to eat. It was especially hard on the small children who needed milk. This was rarely available. The hygienic conditions were beyond description. Except for the bucket in the corner which was covered with a blanket, there was nothing.

After a week the first children died. For the concerned parents the inconceivable came true: They had to bury their dead child beside the railway track, and leave it behind in the anonymous endlessness. When the train moved on, one mother's world collapsed. It was obvious she'd never be able to stand at her child's grave again. There was no place to mourn. Just this never-ending land in which one was lost. And once one was lost, one would never be found again. So, too, the graves of the children would never be found again. Besides, there was no time to mourn. Only the everyday struggle to survive. It wasn't so much a matter of individual survival, since dying could be considered a welcome release. One had to go on living, so that the children were not lost.

On that bright and sunny day when Serafine had to bury her oldest daughter beside the rail line, she spoke not a word – same with the next day. Her mother-in-law Christine, her sister-in-law Martha and Caroline Gehrmann looked after her other children, Natalie and Gottfried. Serafine just sat there staring at the scenery passing by without actually seeing it. She had separated herself from her environment. Nobody knew where she was. Of course, everybody understood. And everyone thought she was with her dead daughter. But nobody really knew and never would know. On the third day, finally, she was back again, looking after her children, preparing meals and shouted at a soldier to kindly give them better support. However, for the rest of her life, she never again mentioned the death of her oldest daughter.

I have no idea how to reach Serafine, thought Christine. *She hasn't spoken for three days. I can understand that. Now she's with us again, but there's something different about her. She fought so hard for her children, and yet she lost one. I hope that time will heal this deep wound. Some scars will remain, of course, but all of us have them. It's important that she regains her courage. She bolstered everyone up with her prayers and wise words. There are people who are clever, some even wise. But what's special about Serafine is that she carries her wisdom in the heart. I can well understand that this heart has been broken. So is mine. However, Serafine's injuries seem so deep that it scares me. Thank God she's talking and taking part in life. But, she doesn't talk about her pain and her loss. Moreover, she doesn't cry any more. Maybe I'm worrying too much about this, and she'll come around soon. She must become her old self again. We need her.*

"I don't know why God allows any of this at all," said Serafine's mother, Pauline, as she, her daughter and Christine sat together with their backs leaning against the wall of the train car. Nobody around them said a word. Some lay on the ground. Many people weren't well in that bake oven, suffering not only from the stuffy air and heat, but also from not knowing when the ordeal would end.

"They've expelled us from our homeland, and now here we are, sitting and not knowing what to expect. Little Auguste has died like many others. One could have doubts about God."

After a while Serafine answered: "It's not God who expelled us. It's not God who's doing all this to us. It's people."

"These damned soldiers, Cossack riff-raff...," a man who had followed the conversation remarked.

"No, these soldiers are not the ones to blame either – whether they're Cossacks or not," replied Serafine. "If they didn't do as they had been told, they'd get killed too. It's the fault of those people who think up such things. Emperors and kings, governments, generals... I don't know... whoever else devises such atrocities."

"One should put this royal and noble riff-raff against the wall then!" roared the man. "There's unrest throughout Russia. The people without land, the small farmers and the factory workers are fed up with being treated so badly. We had it good in Volhynia for a long time. Almost all of us had their own farm. However, there's been a lot of misery throughout Russia. They'll be after the 'fine gentlemen' soon. The revolution won't be stopped."

"How do you know that these people, once they seize power, don't become exactly like the ones who have been ruling us so far?" asked Serafine.

Thank God, Christine thought, *now she's going to be her old self again.*

"You're completely right, Serafine. With murder and manslaughter one can't build a better world. And you," she now said, directing her words to the man with the revolutionary thoughts, "you should listen to my daughter-in-law. She has more brains than any man I know."

"Ha, you women no doubt plan to someday create your own children, too!"

Now he burst out laughing. Others joined in since, for once in this never-ending boredom, there was some interesting conversation taking place which distracted people from their hopeless misery.

"No," Emil now interrupted. "Don't do that to us! If you like, you women can rule the world. However, I beg you, please don't take away that last bit of fun we men can still have in this world."

Now it was his turn to score by making everybody laugh.

Christine replied: "Don't you be so terribly conceited about your manliness. If that's all you're offering us, I'm sure we'll find a way to please ourselves." The people snorted with laughter until Christine tried to calm them down: "That'll do! Let's end this topic. There are children present."

– 22 –

They'd already been travelling for several weeks. In the last few days, the vegetation became more and more sparse. The few remaining trees steadily became smaller. A desolate landscape, appearing to be completely uninhabited. And there were mosquitoes. Mosquitoes! Millions of them tormented the travellers. Some of the children were so swollen from bites that they could barely see. Emil Gehrmann, who always knew everything, informed his fellow-travellers that they were now north of the Arctic Circle. Until then most people didn't know an Arctic Circle existed, never mind where it was. Then the train stopped at a small railway station and everybody had to get out.

"This is how I always imagined the end of the world would look," said Christine.

"Nah, don't worry," said Emil, "the journey's not over yet. Look, all these teams of horses are no doubt waiting for us."

And that's how it was. The people stowed their meagre belongings and then climbed onto the waiting wagons, which were driven by Russians as well as by some strange-looking people. Serafine said something in Russian to the driver of her wagon, but he gesticulated that he could not understand. Then she tried it in German, Ukrainian, Polish, Yiddish and Plautdietsch. Nothing. The man just happily smiled and didn't understand a word.

"Where have we ended up?" she asked Emil.

They had landed in the far North, on the western edge of the Ural Mountains. Now they continued their journey again by horse and wagon, heading further in a westerly direction towards the area of the Nenets, the Khants, the Komi, the Saami and the Selkups. These were the descendants of people from the Asian room of northern Siberia on the other side of the Urals who had moved into the area hundreds of years ago. There was a lot of empty space here, claimed by no one. Their traditional way of life was based on hunting and fishing and, later, breeding reindeers. Some were nomadic or semi-nomadic, following their herds which, migrating with the seasons, would instinctively know where to find food. The reindeer meat was their food and they used the fur for clothing and warmth. Agriculture had been introduced a few years ago by Russian trappers and those exiled by the tsarist regime, but with only a few frost-free months it hadn't been particularly successful. The population density was so spread out that one could travel for weeks without meeting a single person. The huge double island of Novaja Zemlja, situated in the Kara Sea north of the mainland, accommodated only a few hundred people. The people communicated in about a dozen languages with countless dialects. These languages are related to Finnish, Hungarian, Estonian and Turkish, since the relatives of these Nordic people had migrated in various directions long ago in order to secure their existence. Physically, these people could be compared to Eskimos, Mongols or Chinese. A typical person from this race has a round face, a small nose and narrow slit eyes. Others have rather triangular faces, bigger noses and oval eyes. What they all have in common is the smooth black hair. Europeans who stayed awhile in the area learned to easily distinguish the different ethnic origins.

To the new arrivals, however, these people were the strangest human beings they had ever met. But this fear of being amongst strangers soon dissolved when these people showed their friendship and willingness to help. Their cheerfulness was contagious. Their ability to empathize with the emaciated deportees, and the ease with which they shared what little they had, encouraged the newcomers.

The Tsar's advisers constantly reflected on what to do with this useless land in the cold north. For a long time, the area had been used as a place of exile. Those who had fallen out of favour and were no longer wanted in civilised Russia were sent here to be forgotten. The first arrivals had just been abandoned in the wilderness. The ones who came in summer could consider themselves lucky since they were able to build huts. Those who arrived in the winter were mostly condemned to a frozen death. Only a few managed to come back.

Then, mineral resources were discovered, above all coal and ores. Therefore, the exiled were used as labour, in deplorable conditions, to unearth the treasures. The stream of exiles grew. They were joined by convicted criminals who were accommodated in labour camps. The death toll was so high that the provision of further human material, as these people were cynically called, could hardly keep up with the desired economic outcome. That was to change now with the huge stream of Germans arriving who, in the face of war, couldn't stay in Volhynia anymore. Everybody, including women, old people and older children, was to earn their living. Whoever refused to comply, would simply starve.

Finally, after another week full of unbelievable strain, the group reached the coast of the Kara Sea where most of the local helpers said goodbye. Only a few of them as well as a couple of Cossack soldiers came aboard the ships to escort the expellees to the Jamal peninsula. The most beneficial effect the crossing had on the people was that there were no more mosquitoes. Moreover, there was fish and meat to eat which had been almost entirely off the menu for weeks.

The Jamal peninsula received its new inhabitants with sunshine. The small natural harbour looked as if it didn't usually put up bigger ships, and only a few fishing boats were lying at anchor. Now, the people, once again, had to face another walk several kilometers long. The luggage was loaded onto carts which almost sank into the mud of the thawed permafrost. The place called Bresnuv had quickly been created out of nothing and consisted of a few rows of tiny huts made of stone and clay. Wood, as a raw material, was sparse, and used mainly for cooking and heating. Compared to the houses in their home villages, this place simply looked wretched and far from attractive. However, after such a long journey by horse and wagon, by foot, and squashed in a freight train, everyone yearned for a roof over their head. Now, the dwellings were assigned to the new families. The Gehrmanns with their many children were assigned to a hut which they had to share with some others. Young Martha, her friend Emilie and a seven-year-old girl, Augustine Hartfiel, were put up in a house of a Russian family – and, in this case, it really was a house and not a pathetic hut. Like organ pipes, a crowd of children lined up in front of the house, gazing curiously at the new fellow occupants, while the lady of the house, who introduced herself as Nina, gave the three girls a warm welcome.

"My God," said Christine, "why can't Martha just stay with us?"

Christine, Serafine and the small children were given accommodations directly next door, which for the time being, calmed Christine. Anna, a middle-aged Russian, took her guests in her arms, gave both children a kiss and took the little boy from Serafine. Thus, all the newcomers were divided amongst the dwellings of the settlement without any noticeable disapproval from the inhabitants. On the contrary, the friendliness and thoughtfulness of the locals was the greatest joy they had experienced in many weeks.

– 23 –

The hut in which Christine and Serafine now had to live consisted of a kitchen with a stove, a primitive, badly constructed table, and wooden benches, as well as a bedroom divided from the kitchen with a curtain. There was a big bed and a bench for sleeping. After the children were provided for and put to sleep, the three women – Anna, Serafine and Christine – sat at the table eating bortsch with reindeer meat.

"I'm so glad," said Serafine to Anna, "that we've finally reached our destination and, of course, that you've accepted us so warmly. I was starting to think that this journey would never end. If things had continued like they were, we all would have died."

"I know what it's like, Serafine," replied Anna. "I, too, have this journey behind me. Three years ago, my husband was exiled to this place. Since I didn't want to leave him alone, I took my son and came too. However, my son, Alexej, never survived the strenuous trip. He died along the way. Then, two years ago, I gave birth to a girl. But she didn't live long either. Finally, my husband died half a year ago. And now I'm stuck here and don't have any money for the return journey. I work at the glass factory and it is long drudgery. I hope I can return some day. I come from the Orenburg area. It's a wonderful place – especially the climate… When the fire goes out here in the winter, it is so cold; one could freeze to death in the house. I'm so glad you're here with me now. Now the fire won't ever go out, because I'm in good company and finally have children around me again."

"It's also a wonderful place," said Christine, "where we come from. Volhynia is in the Ukraine. Everything you can ever imagine grows there. When I think of the cherry trees my heart feels warm."

"You'll never get to see cherries up here, that's for sure. Instead, there's reindeer meat and fish. During the short summers a few vegetables grow, mostly cabbage, which we preserve for the winter. Anyway, we don't starve up here. You have to get along well with the Nenets, of course, since they supply us with meat. It's not much you can buy in the store. It's just too long a journey up to here in the north. And now that there's a war, there's even less reaching us."

In the house next door Nina, Martha and her friend Emilie, who was the same age, sat together at the kitchen table and talked. Nina's seven children and Augustine were already sleeping in the adjoining room.

"Where is your husband?" Martha asked Nina.

"He's working. He's transporting glass, which is produced in the local factory, to the harbour or to the freight train station. Sometimes he doesn't come home for a couple of days. And then, when he's here, he's so exhausted that he just sleeps. And when he's not sleeping, he's busy creating new life. He always manages to have enough energy for that, inspite of his exhaustion."

They all started to giggle.

"But you already have so many children," Emilie said with amazement.

"I've had more, but some have died... such is life."

Now Nina told her story. She came from southern Russia in the vicinity of Saratov. Her parents had many children, more than they could nourish. Her father worked mostly as a day labourer for farmers. At times, the family didn't even have a halfway inhabitable house. They lived in mud shacks with roofs made of branches and brushwood. At the age of twelve, Nina was handed over to a farmer's family to help with the housework, because the wife was ill and could barely manage to look after her two small children. When she was sixteen, she got to know Michail, a young man with whom she fell in love. He could work hard and had plans. When he volunteered to work in the far north, she was already expecting their first child. Nina had sworn to herself to provide for her children so they would never be sent to strangers or have to live in mud shacks. And, so far, she has succeeded. Michail worked hard. Though living up here wasn't easy, they had always managed to have enough to eat for the growing family. The wages here in the north were higher than in other parts of Russia.

"And now I've even got two extra helpers," she said. "You'll certainly work in the glass factory. If you contribute a bit to the housekeeping money and lend me a hand here and there, then I make sure you're always well fed, have a place to sleep, and also a bit of fun. Together, we'll withstand this long winter, in which there's barely any light for months on end, much better. By the way, what's the matter with little Augustine? She seems to be very sad."

"Her mother died while we were travelling," said Martha. "Then, a little later, also her older brother. Now she has no one. She hardly spoke a word for the rest of the trip. But she trusts us and cuddles up to me."

"Yes, life can be cruel," answered Nina. "I think, being here amongst all the children she will thaw out again. I'll simply treat her as if she was my own daughter."

Martha and Emilie were glad to be with this cheerful woman who herself was hardly thirty years old. Her optimism and energy made the future look a little brighter again.

Lord, I'm grateful that this journey is finally over, Serafine prayed in her thoughts while she was lying in bed together with her mother-in-law and the two children. As Anna had insisted that they take the bed, she herself put up with the narrow and rather uncomfortable bench for sleeping. *Thank you,* Serafine continued to pray, *for letting us stay with this fine woman. Thank you for letting us eat our fill today, and, after all those terrible weeks in the wagon, thank you for again giving us a bed to sleep in.* Deeply exhausted, she fell asleep.

– 24 –

Life was hard in the far north. But after all the people had been through during the long journey, at least they had a chance for a certain routine again. They had a place to sleep and they could wash themselves properly. Admittedly, the food was unusual at first, but no one had to starve. The symptoms of malnourishment which had surfaced near the end of the journey could now be quickly remedied. And there was work. Hard work. Many women worked in the glass factory. Since somebody had to look after the children, one woman in the neighbourhood would stay at home. She'd have to be supported by the others. Serafine insisted that Christine was to remain in the house. She wouldn't allow her mother-in-law to work in the factory at her age – now that she was in her early fifties. Thus, every morning a few other children joined her own. Christine looked after them, kept the house, prepared the meals and did the laundry. She taught the bigger ones reading and writing and told stories to the little ones. Serafine and Anna went together to the glass factory. They'd be away for thirteen hours every day, which included the trip there and back, as well as two short breaks, six days a week.

They were unaccustomed to the winter. Even in Volhynia it could get ice cold. But after some time the weather would change and temperatures would become rather mild again. Here, however, it was a constant deep freeze. Minus thirty degrees was considered mild. Most of the time it was between forty and fifty degrees below zero. Add to this the constant darkness. There was never any real light. Months of darkness. It wasn't good for one's soul.

"My goodness, will the sun ever shine again? I almost have the impression that it's fallen from the sky and we're not going to see it again for the rest of our lives," Serafine said to Anna.

"Don't worry, it'll come back again. The most important thing, during this darkness, is not to be alone – otherwise you'll go to pieces! It's best to always have some company. Then you won't become melancholy."

Some men worked in the mines. This was especially hard. The underground working conditions were beyond description. For farmers who were used to working in the fields and looking out to the horizon, it was hell. It was worse than hell for those workers who were also prisoners. After having worked one's shift, a normal worker could go home, wash himself, eat, spend his time in a heated place and go to bed. Prisoners, however, only had their cold cells in which, during the winter, ice covered the walls. Their skin was black; every pore plugged. They rarely had an opportunity to wash themselves. Their meals consisted of thin soup and a crust of bread. The little they were entitled to, was eaten by the guards. Most supervisors hadn't come up here voluntarily either, and were kept on a tight leash as well.

The men who could work outdoors were better off than the mineworkers. Though one was exposed to the murderous cold and always had to watch for frostbite, but at least it didn't feel like hell.

The winter of 1916/17 was especially hard, not only up here in the north. All of Russia had become a gigantic freezer. In addition, war had claimed more and more victims. Russia was starving. Barely any food reached the north. The trains brought only more prisoners who had fallen victim to the political purge of the tsarist regime. With the scarcity of food in the work camps almost all the condemned were doomed to die.

In February 1917, spontaneous violence broke out in Russia. Either one starved, or one got shot by the government authorities during a protest. These hunger revolts soon developed a momentum of their own. Political power was slipping through the fingers of the regime. Finally, Tsar Nicolaus II had to resign and went into exile with his family, near the area of Yekaterinburg in Siberia.

"Have you heard? The Tsar has been overthrown," Martha said totally excited. She rushed into Anna's house, took off her thick clothes and sat down. Anna, Christine and Serafine stared at her in disbelief.

"How do you know this?" asked Christine.

"Nina's husband brought a newspaper. It's already few weeks old. But I don't think he'll ever be claiming the throne again. Now, there's a Duma government. Probably, there will never be a Tsar again."

"I'm wondering if this will bring the desired changes," asked Serafine doubtfully.

"Something must change," answered Christine.

"Things can't keep on like this."

"It's rumbling all over the country. People have been taking to the streets demanding more to eat and better working conditions," said Martha.

"I hope they won't get disappointed," replied Serafine, as she lifted her son carefully from her lap to the floor.

"By the way," said Martha, now smiling and taking on a straight posture. "The more important news is that Fred and I are going to get married."

Now the three other women could not shut their mouths.

Russia 1918/1919

– 25 –

"We Germans are said to be diligent and good workers," said Serafine to Anna, the woman with whom she, her children, and mother-in-law Christine had been staying with since 1915. "But what the people must achieve here is almost unbelievable."

"And we're relatively well off," answered Anna. "If you ever looked inside a penal camp, you'd have nightmares for the rest of your life. The people work twelve hours a day in the mine – day after day with only a little break. There's only a thin soup to eat and, when available, a piece of bread. They live in tiny cells which are so cold that ice forms on the walls. They don't have proper facilities to wash themselves. Coal dust penetrates their skin so deeply, one might think these people are Negros. Everybody is ill. Many have tuberculosis. And then the bugs! Lice, bed bugs, fleas. The minimum sentence is ten years. Ten years under such conditions is a death sentence. Hardly anybody withstands it. Most people die within the first three years. – That's why I say, compared to all that, we're still well off, although I long to get away from here."

"Whatever someone might have done, one can't treat people like this."

"These people have usually done nothing," answered Anna with outrage. "It's enough just to be politically conspicuous, just by expressing one's opinion. We, the little people, are simply material for the high and mighty. If we're of no more use for them at home, then they send us here where we're exploited to our last breath. And then we're kindly supposed to die, because there are enough to take our place."

"You're talking like a revolutionary, Anna."

"It's high time people went on the warpath. Though I have my doubts that this will change much. So far, the revolutionaries treat people just like their predecessors did. Look at those who have been sent here lately. These people aren't criminals. And the way these people talk about what's happening down south. Obviously, all hell has been let loose there."

"I don't understand what Russia has become," said Serafine. "We used to live such a good life here. When I think back on my childhood almost everyone was doing well. And those who had problems were supported. I don't know what it was like in the big cities, but in the villages, life was wonderful. After all that has happened in the meantime, I don't think things will ever be the same again. As soon as I can get away from here, I'm going to Germany with my children."

Now Anna looked sad, because a separation from her friend and the children would be difficult. Besides, she herself didn't have the option of simply leaving.

"I'm going over to Nina's place now," said Serafine. "Today it's my turn to read the Bible to the children and teach them their writing. I'm just happy that we now have slates; it's impossible to get hold of any paper."

"Tell me one thing that isn't hard to get hold of! There have been hardly any goods sent to us from the south. We can only be glad that the locals still supply us with meat, although we hardly have anything to give in exchange; and for the few roubles we pay them they can't buy anything proper in the store."

– 26 –

"I want to get out of here as soon as possible," Serafine said to Katlika. The two sat with Martha at the kitchen table in Serafine's lodging.

"Who doesn't?" answered Katlika. "The only problem is that it's very expensive to return to Volhynia."

"Who's speaking of Volhynia anyway? I don't want go there again. Nobody's waiting for me there. My husband is dead, my parents are buried here in this cold soil. And I think my sisters would also rather head for Germany."

"To Germany?" Katlika stared at Serafine in astonishment. "How on earth are you going to get there? It'll cost a fortune. Besides, you don't know whether they'd even let you go."

"No matter what, I have to go to Moscow and put in an application. The German embassy there might help. Also, I've read that we have permission to travel freely again. Whoever wants to return to Volhynia or go somewhere else can do so according to the armistice agreement between Germany and Russia. I've written to relatives in Germany asking if they can help me out by sending me some money."

"And did you get an answer?"

"No, I'm not sure whether my letters arrived. But that doesn't make a difference. Somehow, I'll make my way. I just don't see a future for us here in Russia. First the war and now this revolution. One gets the impression that everybody's fighting each other. Who knows what to expect back in Volhynia? Maybe our houses don't exist anymore, or other people are living in them and won't give them back to us."

"Hmm, I can hardly imagine this," said Katlika. "Eduard and I definitely want to go back to Volhynia as soon as possible. Once we have babies again, they'll have a good chance to survive there."

Here in the north, Katlika had given birth to two children, who had both died. During their three years' stay, many people had died. It was worst for the inmates of the labour camps. They received the worst provisions, froze the most, and worked the hardest. A steady stream of prisoners was sent up north to keep the area from becoming depopulated and to stop the mines and adjoining factories from grinding to a standstill. Like their predecessors, those currently in power kept sending prisoners to penal camps and other undesirables to exile. The system of dealing with alleged enemies remained the same. The horrors remained.

The door opened and in came Pauline, the wife of Serafine's brother Rudolf.

"Well, the right ones are sitting together already," said Pauline as she took off her boots and the heavily insulated jacket. "It only takes a fifteen minute-walk to get chilled to the bone."

"We've been talking about going home," said Katlika.

"Well," said Pauline, "where is home anyway? We don't know if our houses are still there. As far as I'm concerned, I'd only return to Volhynia to search for Rudolf. Maybe he's already there waiting for us. Who knows if we'd be allowed to remain in Volhynia and would we want to, even if we could. The whole world has gone crazy. Up here, we don't hear or see much; but, supposedly, there's civil war everywhere. There's no Tsar any more. And will those, who are now in power, leave us in peace? I'm not sure."

"I can understand why you have to go to Volhynia," said Serafine. "But I don't want to go there any more. I'm setting off for Germany. And Martha wants to go to Poland."

Martha, Katlika's younger sister, had got married here. Originally, Alfred Brandt had come from Poland and just happened to be in Janowka when they'd started to send the Germans away. Because the Russians hadn't allowed him to return home, he'd also ended up in the far north where he got to know Martha who now had a one-year-old son, Alfred junior. Unfortunately, her husband died shortly before the child's birth, but she had promised him to travel to Poland to visit his parents or maybe even start a new life there.

Now Martha indicated her wish to speak:

"I'll take Augustine with me, since she's become like a daughter to me. Emilie wants to come along, too, because there's nobody left in Volhynia waiting for her."

The door opened again and in came Christine.

"Please quickly pour me in a cup of hot tea," she said while she peeled off her bulky clothes. Completely out of breath, she sat down asking: "Are you making plans again about who's going where?"

"Of course," answered Katlika, "it's just about time since the first transport to the south is due to leave in two weeks. The bay has already frozen over, and the nearest railway station isn't as far away as it was three years ago."

"But don't forget this murderous cold and the little children!" said Christine.

"Sure, but in the spring there'll be mud everywhere," replied Serafine. "We should get out of here as soon as possible. Who knows if they'll even let us go later on."

"But it's just so stupid that we're all going to be scattered to the four corners of the earth," said Christine while she tugged at her hair which had greyed in the last few years.

"Serafine wants to go to Germany, Martha to Poland. At least, you'll come with me to Volhynia, Katlika and Pauline. As far as I'm concerned, I must return to Janowka. What if Gottlieb goes home and nobody's there?"

Christine seemed to have reached the end of her strength.

Again the door opened. This time Anna, the owner of the small hut, entered.

"Damn it! Who invented this terrible cold? And then this wind, too!"

After she had taken off her jacket and shoes, she glanced at the pot on the stove, in which a soup was slowly simmering. She inhaled the aroma with great relish and said:

"So, you women sit here in my little house and hatch plans on how to leave me in the lurch as quickly as possible. What am I going to do without you? I can't stand the thought that soon there won't be any children around either. I'm going to die of loneliness."

"Just come with us, then," said Christine. "There's enough room in my house."

"Christine, you don't seriously think that they'd let me leave here, do you? Who knows what's happening in your home village? Maybe the Bolsheviks are controlling the area. No matter who's in charge, they'll find a way to keep the little people small. The big lords come and go, but for us, everything remains the same."

Nobody wanted to contradict Anna, the good-hearted soul, but each woman had her own glimmer of hope towards a better future.

Just like in the house of Christine and Serafine, people everywhere were discussing the same affairs these days. The war came to an end and the Germans from Volhynia were allowed to go home. Nobody considered staying in this inhospitable north. However, there were many who were ill or too weak to undertake such a murderous journey. There were also people who simply had no means at all, for example if they couldn't work because of poor health. Others, on the other hand, wanted to wait until the summer.

Of course, the journey home was also the topic under discussion at Gehrmann's. Emil, the head of the family, was absolutely convinced that he and his wife Caroline, together with their swarm of, now eight children, would leave as soon as possible. Their farmstead in Volhynia would provide a much better living for the family than paid labour did up here. Emil had always been his own master. Besides, what he could buy here for his hard-earned money was barely enough. Too little to live on, too much to die from. Sometimes, however, it was enough to die. There was no healthcare, school only through private initiative, and since there was no church, services were held in private homes. This wasn't the life that he and Caroline had envisioned for their children.

"So, we'll take the first train that's going south. If our house still stands, that's good. If it doesn't, we'll build another one. Everything's settled."

At the end of November, 1918, a trek of about thirty teams started on their way.They crossed the frozen bay to the east of the peninsula, heading for the railway station. The cold took people's breath away, but seemed to make no difference to the locals and the reindeer that pulled their sleighs. Without the help and knowledge of these people, the whole venture would have failed after one or two days. The Nenets and the Khants knew how to survive in this climate. And so, after a few days, thanks to the frozen ground and lack of heavy snow, they reached their destination. It was a great stroke of luck that the train was already waiting for them. However, that finished their allotment of luck. The rest of the journey would be dreadful.

– 27 –

The train was more comfortable than the one they'd travelled on in the opposite direction three and a half years ago. There were wooden benches for everybody. The freight cars, trailing the passenger coaches, were full of raw materials from the north. The people brought smoked meat and dried fish for the journey. There were no potatoes and vegetables. The bread, made of the scarce stocks of flour, was already used up. Buying food along the way was only possible much further to the south where the bigger towns were located. One dared not think of milk for the children. A woman who couldn't nurse her own baby had to rely on the support and sympathy of other breastfeeding mothers.

After two days at slow throttle there were massive snowdrifts blocking the railway tracks. The men had to get out and shovel. It never stopped. The snow fell incessantly and the train crawled forward at a snail's pace. While there were little stoves heated with wood, it got increasingly colder in the coaches. All were at the mercy of this white endlessness. The initial excited departing atmosphere turned into an oppressive fear of never reaching the end of the journey, doomed in this vast expanse of land, to starve and freeze to death, and to never see their home again.

Home… what did that actually mean?

Volhynia with its rich grain fields, fat cows and the sour cherry trees? Martha dreamed of Poland; her late husband Alfred had never tired of describing his native country in the nicest summer colours. Serafine thought about Germany which she'd never seen. However, she pictured a good future there for herself and her children. Despite all the confusion, a few days before their departure, she'd received a letter from Germany. Some relatives from Mecklenburg had answered her letter and invited her to come. They'd even enclosed some money, although life in Germany must have been difficult after the war. But that's what families were there for. However, first she had to escape this white chaos and then somehow make her way to Moscow. From there she would try and get a train to Poland and then on to Germany. If that wasn't possible, she could go to Petrograd and from there take a ship to Germany, assuming there were ships, and the Baltic was free of ice. Otherwise, she'd have to wait and simply make the best of things during the intervening period. She thanked God that at least her sister Auguste would stay with her. Her other sister, Augustine, wanted to return to Volhynia with her children, hoping to reunite with her husband. Whatever one did or planned to do, it was a journey into the unknown. The ifs and buts were countless. Yet one needed an aim or else one was completely lost.

– 28 –

Tragedy began when Katlika's husband Eduard collapsed while shovelling snow and had to be carried onto the train. His body burned with fever, his muscles ached, he could barely speak, and he had intense shivers. Because he kept slipping off the bench, Katlika finally set up a makeshift camp of rugs and furskins on the floor, with the result that nobody could walk by anymore. Although they constantly poured hot tea into his mouth, covered him with everything available within reach, he continued to shake with paroxysms of cold. When a soldier entered the compartment, shouting at Katlika that she ought not block the passageway, tempers flared and Katlika ended up calling the army man a *shithead*! She said it in German, but the soldier turned around as he was leaving.

"I understood that."

She couldn't care less. All she cared about was her husband's health.

The next day, with the train moving only a few kilometers, two similar cases occurred amongst the passengers. People became increasingly worried. The disaster took its course.

It had started in May in Spain. Within a few months up to eight million people had died of influenza. It mostly affected the twenty to forty-year-old age group. Then, the illness flickered repeatedly in various areas all around the globe and took its victims. By 1920, more than twenty-five million people would die of that flu. That was more than all the battles of the world war had claimed. Other sources speak of nearly fifty million deaths.

In the next ten days a large number of passengers became seriously ill. First, Eduard died, followed by Caroline Gehrmann and her four youngest children. By the time the train arrived in Rostow-on-Don, one quarter of all the people had died. It wasn't just the sickness itself, but also the lack of nourishment that wore the people down, making it impossible for them to fight the deadly virus.

Serafine, her two children, Natalie and Gottfried, as well as her sister Auguste got off the train here to continue their journey to Moscow. Saying goodbye to her sister Augustine, her sister-in-law Pauline, and her mother-in-law Christine was hard. Saying goodbye to her sister-in-law, Katlika – who'd just lost her husband – was especially heart-wrenching. It had been Katlika who had stood by her after Friedrich's death. And now she had to let this young widow travel on alone. Taking leave from Martha, her late husband's other sister, wasn't easy either. At least, Martha had her son as well as her good friend Emilie and ten-year-old Wilhelmine. Certainly, they would do fine in Poland.

Some people on the train wanted to take their relatives to a hospital in Rostow-on-Don. But at the railway station they were told it was pointless. All hospitals were already overcrowded with war invalids, and now there was this wave of influenza. There were no beds available, no medicine, and not enough doctors. The station master told the conductor to leave the railway station as soon as possible, or he would order soldiers to force them on. It would be best for the passengers to move on as far away as possible. Maybe circumstances were better somewhere else. Shopping was also out of the question. There was nothing left to buy. Because of the ravages of war, of lootings, of uncultivated fields, of the onset of winter which, for December, was unusually harsh, of the many injured and mutilated soldiers, of the effects of the revolution, of all the people who were on the move, of the homeless and the displaced, of those newly impoverished by the revolution, and of those who never owned anything and never would – because of all this, they were heading directly towards a famine.

Serafine was happy when she, her children and her sister were on a train bound for Moscow. Though the future was uncertain, she at least had a goal.

Dear mother-in-law Christine, thought Serafine, *if only you knew how difficult it's been to leave you. I'm praying for you, hoping that your son Gottlieb is waiting at home when you arrive in Volhynia. At least, Katlika is staying with you. I'm sure you two women will manage to build yourselves a proper life again very soon. And you, dear Katlika, when you've done grieving, will most certainly find another man and start a new family with him. Oh Martha, little Martha, hopefully you'll be happy in Poland. What will your parents-in-law say when they hear their son is dead? And how surprised they'll be when they see their grandchild!*

Serafine sat, deep in thought, on a wooden bench heading towards Moscow. She conversed with the people she had just left behind, especially those three courageous women – Christine, Katlika and Martha – who had been so dear to her that having to let them go on their own almost broke her heart. Only the fact that she had two children to care for relieved her pain. In her heart of hearts, she knew Volhynia didn't hold a future for her children. Therefore, she had to go to Germany. Even if that meant she'd never see her husband's grave again. It was also uncertain, whether she'd ever see the three women again who were on their way to Volhynia.

– 29 –

"I've told you five times now that I'm German, possess a Russian passport, that my husband served in the Russian army and was killed in action, that I was born in Volhynia, that my children and sister are Germans, and that we want to travel to Germany," said Serafine to the official at the foreign affairs office in Moscow.

"But now the Party rules, and it's the Party that decides who travels to Germany and who stays here."

"I've given you the papers from the German embassy. According to the treaty agreed upon by both countries, I have the right to go to Germany."

"Who has what rights is decided by the Party. And the Party has authorized me to decide on its behalf. If you want a quick decision, there's a lot of effort and cost involved."

Serafine now understood.

"And how much is the fee?"

"It depends… two adults, two children..."

Serafine made a grab for her bag, got out a few notes and pushed them over the counter to the official.

"This is all I have."

The man took the money and disappeared through the door. After a few minutes he came back with a form, filled it out, stamped it and handed it to Serafine with a smile.

"It's simply my good nature. I could have sent you back to Volhynia to get approval first. Then you could have returned to Moscow, and then I would have stamped it. I'm just feeling some pity for poor women and fatherless children."

"Thank you very much," she replied, feeling a heavy weight lifting from her heart.

The journey from Rostow-on-Don to Moscow was not without danger. At every railway station soldiers boarded the train to check passengers for whatever reason. A few times people were roughly taken away. Almost every time they were questioned about who they were, where they were from and where they wanted to go. But two women travelling with two small children appeared too harmless to get into real difficulties. The journey lasted almost one week, because the train sometimes didn't move for hours; sometimes even for a whole night.

Finding a lodging in Moscow, this endless big city, turned out to be much more difficult. Finally, for a small fee, they found a place to rest in a ransacked church. The next day they set off for the German embassy which had been moved from Petrograd to Moscow. After a long wait, first in front of, and then inside the building, they received the necessary documents which they then brought to the Russian foreign affairs office. Back at the railway station, they found out that there were no more trains going to Germany, only one to Warsaw. Since nobody could tell them when that train would depart, they decided to wait at the station.

They waited two days and two nights. When the train started slowly moving, Serafine said to her sister: "It's hard to believe, but we really have made it. What day is today, anyway?"

"Today's the 25th of December – my God, it's Christmas! Isn't this a wonderful Christmas present?"

"Yes," answered Serafine, "and the best part is we've all stayed healthy. When I think of all the dead since we left the end of the world. And who knows, maybe that disease is still raging. I'm so sorry about all that. I pray to God that the others reach their destination safe and sound, whether it's Volhynia, Poland or Germany."

"Why didn't Martha come with us? She could have taken this train, too," asked Auguste.

"I think, she still wanted to stay a little while with her mother and her sister and see how things are in Volhynia. Also, she promised her deceased husband to show their child to his parents. Who knows, maybe everything will get better for Martha in Poland."

– 30 –

By the time the train, which came from the far north, reached Kiev, more people became ill and died. Together with the influenza came other diseases, especially intestinal infections and fleck typhus. Nutritional deficiency, exhaustion and poor hygienic conditions made people prone to diseases. For the survivors, the worst of it was, that at temperatures below minus thirty degrees, no graves could be dug. The bodies were stored in freight wagons to be buried later, sometime and somewhere, without dignity, probably in mass graves.

Shortly before the train arrived in Kiev, Martha, Katlika and Christine sat together with Emil Gehrmann discussing how to proceed. Despite the heavy loss he suffered with the death of his wife and four youngest children, Emil hadn't lost his practical sensibility: "Like everybody else from Janowka and Solomiak, we must pool our money to buy one or more horses and wagons, buy some provisions for the journey and then get moving. I'm afraid, though, that most people will have to walk. The main thing is, we let the little ones, the old and the sick ride."

"Moving is good when it's cold as this," said Katlika.

"We must find people along the way who will let us spend a night in their stable and prepare a warm meal for ourselves," said Christine.

"Poor people are helpful. And in this country, people are, for the most part, poor by now," replied Emil.

"No matter what, we should be confident about the future," suggested Martha. "After all we've come through, we'll also manage the rest."

Finally, a group of forty people formed and set off in a westerly direction. Their destination: Janowka. It wasn't possible to get horse and wagons in Kiev, so in the end, everybody had to walk, taking turns to carry the small children and support the aged and infirm. At least, it wasn't as cold as it had been, even though it was now January. In the evening they reached a farmstead outside of Kiev which was occupied by soldiers.

"These are Reds," said Emil Gehrmann to Christine. "They're making the revolution. And because the revolution is for the poor and landless classes, we've come to the right place. Let's go and see whether they'll help us."

After Emil and his friend Julius negotiated with the soldiers, the group was assigned the pigsty which had not one single animal in it. They covered the ground with straw. And they were even given a few cabbages and some bacon to cook a soup.

The next day, after payment, they received two sleighs with a horse for each. Now, the small children and the sick no longer had to walk.

"How Emil always manages everything so well," Katlika said to her mother.

"The man has a natural talent when it comes to organizing," she answered.

However, there was still a long way ahead of them. Soon, no one paid attention to what was actually happening in this country, who was in authority or not, who was friend or foe. They met soldiers belonging to the Whites and then those defending the independence of the Ukraine. They met Cossacks who fought for or against the Tsar's regime, for or against the revolution. There were soldiers from Romania, from the Bukovina and even a group of Greeks who had formed an alliance with them. Far in the west, close to the area which they used to call their homeland, they met the Polish army defending Western Ukraine on behalf of Poland.

"I thought the war's over long ago," said Christine in amazement.

"That's right," answered Emil, "but now the struggle for power over the Ukraine is in full swing. Everybody wants a piece of the cake, only the Ukrainians get nothing. It's been like that over the centuries, and it'll be like that now. However the whole situation ends, the Ukrainians, and probably us, too, will be in deep shit. No matter what we do for this country, our presence is only tolerated at best, but we are not welcome."

My God, I'm so excited, thought Katlika. *First, we'll heat Mother's house properly, wash ourselves and make the beds. Then we must find something to eat. And then we'll make ourselves really comfortable. Home sweet home! Even if the house is perhaps in a bad shape, we're going to have a roof over our heads again. And in spring we'll get the garden in shape again… and the fields. We'll make it! Somehow it will be like it used to be. Of course, it hurts without Eduard, and all the others who have died. Nevertheless, let's get down to it now and think of the future. Too bad Serafine isn't with us. I've grown very fond of her little ones. And Martha, well, there's still time for her to reconsider and not go to Poland.*

Living in the house without Karl and Serafine will be hard, Christine thought. *Above all, I really miss the two children, Natalie and Gottfried. But, at least, I can visit the graves of Karl and Friedrich again. I pray to God that my second son, Gottlieb, will be there. The war is over. He simply must be alive. And if he lives, he's bound to be at home. Where else would he go?*

Thus, everyone on the way to Janowka had his or her dreams. Those who'd been to hell and lost so many loved ones and then returned home after such a long time, were more than likely to picture the future as bright and beautiful, for everything is better than hell. But there was also fear that not all their dreams would come true. Nobody could know all that had happened in the meantime.

– 31 –

Three and a half years ago, the people had left a flourishing village. Flourishing, in spite of war and all the forced taxes and ransackings. The waving grain fields had almost cried to be harvested. It had broken people's hearts to look at their village from the opposite bank of the river. Had it been an ugly, miserable place, it might not have been so difficult. But it was the beauty of this small village with its fruit trees, its flowers in front of the houses, its gardens, its pastures and fields framed by the woodlands. It made their hearts heavy. During those difficult years in the inhospitable north, it had been the picture of this summery rich village which had kept people longing for home and the domestic bliss they had lost. They simply believed that once they were home, everything would be good again. The picture that they now saw, had nothing in common with the pleasant memories of that special place. Some couldn't even recognize their own village or house. This couldn't be blamed on winter. When the people lived here before, there'd been winter and had wonderful memories associated with it. Snow-covered fields, sun-flooded white splendor, skating on the frozen river, comfortable, warm houses, the prayer house filled with candles, Christmas with the family – that's what winters used to be like in Janowka. Compared to that, it was now a picture of misery. The group crept along the main road, not believing that this could be their village. Roofs were repaired in a makeshift way, window panes were not replaced by glass, but by cardboard or wood. Only a few chimneys appeared to be working properly. There was no smell of livestock, nobody crossing the main street to say hello. Janowka seemed like a ghost town. When Christine stopped at her front door, a middle-aged woman opened and asked:

"What do you want here?"

Christine was absolutely baffled by the situation. Behind her stood Katlika and Martha looking at each other like they could no longer understand the world. Utterly amazed, Emil stood there on the road, his hands on his hips and yelled:

"This is my house! What do you want here?"

Now the woman started getting angry, scolding them in Polish: "Bloody German rabble! Who do you think you are? You think you can drop everything and then come back and take my house away? Go back where you came from."

Then she slammed the door.

"I don't believe this!" said Christine.

Poland 1919

– 32 –

In view of the unfriendly welcome in Volhynia, Martha, along with her young son, Emilie and Ausgustine, decided to proceed to Poland as soon as possible. Like the Exners, almost all the families returning to Janowka had similar experiences. The few houses that weren't inhabited by others, had been plundered to the last chair and cup.

It turned out that Emil Litke, a handsome man in his early thirties who had survived the war without injury, decided to set off for Poland soon, along with his parents. By coincidence, they were going to the Gostynin area, which was where Martha was also heading. Originally, the Litkes had come from Mokro-Polskie, a small town near Gostynin. They'd been living in Volhynia for many years, but now it was almost impossible to earn a living here. They were hoping for better living conditions in Poland. And if things didn't work out there, they'd move on to Pomerania where the Litkes had some relatives. Anything was better than staying here and watching other people living in their house. There was no more livestock; and there was a possibility they wouldn't be allowed to cultivate their own fields. How was one supposed to support one's self?

Emil Litke organized a horse-drawn sleigh trip which, in four days, brought them to Lublin where they boarded a train to Warsaw. Then, after a one day wait, they proceeded to Gostynin. The village in which Martha's in-laws lived was only one and a half hours away from the Litke family's destination. Emil again got them all a sleigh, and after he dropped his parents off at Mokro-Polskie where they stayed with some relatives, he then travelled on with Martha, her son, Emilie and Augustine. It was agreed that Emil would drop in at Martha's in-laws in a couple of days to check and make sure everything was all right. During their trip together, Martha and Emil became attracted to each other. Martha's husband had been dead for over a year now, and it had never occurred to her that she'd be able to look at another man again. But when she looked into Emil's eyes, she was filled with a feeling that she hadn't felt for a long time.

Marthas parents-in-law had last seen their son almost four years ago. They didn't know he had been sent to the most northerly point of Russia. His letters had not reached them. They also didn't know – how could they? – that he'd gotten married and they'd become grandparents. And, finally, they didn't know that he was dead.

Emil had dropped off Martha, her little son Fred, Emilie and Augustine in front of the farmhouse of the Brandts. Since it was getting dark already, he immediately set off for his parents again. The door opened and out came a woman wearing an apron, and a man in his work clothes. Martha approached them saying: "Good afternoon, I am Martha Brandt. I was married to your son and I'm bringing you your grandchild."

The woman stared at Martha like she was paralyzed. At least her husband appeared able to think straight. He looked at the small boy in Martha's arms and asked: "Is Alfred dead?"

"Yes."

Now, Alfred's mother couldn't control herself anymore. She started screaming: "Oh God, I knew it. Why? Why now, too, our last son?"

After the situation became more calm, they all sat down together in the kitchen. Rosina, Martha's mother-in-law, put little Alfred on her lap and fed him porridge. She was completely captivated by the little boy, observing even the tiniest movements. On the table there was bread, butter and marmalade – delicacies the guests hadn't seen for a long while.

The father-in-law, named Alfred, said: "We had five children, four died early on. Only Alfred grew up to be a man. His death is a heavy blow to us. That he's left a son behind is quite wonderful."

"You'll be staying with us, won't you?" asked the mother, and Martha answered: "I don't know where I should go. I promised your son on his deathbed that I'd come here and show you your grandchild. Unfortunately, he himself didn't get a chance to get to know his son. He died shortly before the birth."

"We've just endured the heavy blow that Alfred is dead. At the same time, we get to experience the miracle of our own grandchild. You can't just leave again so soon," said Rosina in a voice mixed with hope and despair.

"For the time being, we'll stay here and then we'll see what the future holds. I must look after Augustine, too. I've promised her. And Emilie must also find accommodation somewhere. We've been through so much together."

Thank God, thought Martha as she lay in bed later that evening, *that my in-laws are such nice people.* Martha and her little son had to share the bed that once belonged to her husband. Rosina got two straw mattresses out for Emilie and Pauline who fell into a sound sleep after the exhausting trip. Martha, however, was wide awake. The heavy burden of telling her parents-in-law about their son's death had fallen off her. Of course, they were grief-stricken. But the dear Lord had arranged things so that she brought a great relief and consolation when she introduced little Fred to them. *They're good people,* Martha thought. *Rosina immediately fell in love with her grandson. They set the table without hesitation, willing to share with us the best things they have. It's nice to finally feel welcomed somewhere.*

In the next few days they continued to discuss the future. What remained of this small farm after the war was miserable. It was obvious that the couple could not support four guests indefinitely. Even if everybody worked hard next spring, there wouldn't be enough. Finding work for Martha and Emilie would be difficult, too. In this area, nobody had enough wealth to afford additional eaters or workers. The situation was tense.

Now, they had already been here four weeks. Martha and Emilie made themselves useful whenever possible while Rosina gave little Fred all of her attention. She fed him, and bathed him in the zinc tub in the kitchen. He learnt to walk and speak at breakneck speed and enjoyed his grandmother singing songs to him. Rosina came to life.

She loved this little boy with every fibre of her being. Her husband sometimes stood there, shaking his head: "This little lad has driven my wife out of her mind."

Naturally, he was glad that all the hopelessness, gnawing at her over the past years of uncertainty, had gone. At this time of year, there wasn't much to do anyway. Martha milked the only cow still left in the stable. She also fed the two pigs, one of which would soon be sold and the other one slaughtered. In the evening, after mucking out, she sat down with the spinning wheel. It was less work than she was used to. Emilie was responsible for the housekeeping: washing the laundry, ironing, baking bread, mending the clothes. Both women were accustomed to working much harder. Since the fields didn't need tilling, and fruit and vegetable gardens weren't needing attention, there simply wasn't enough work for four adults. Even ten-year-old Augustine livened up again. Rosina was very good to her. Sometimes, to her delight, she even let her look after her grandson.

"Who would ever have thought that we'd have a grandchild?"

Rosina sat with her husband at the kitchen table with little Fred on her lap.

"I didn't believe anything any more," answered her husband. "I thought, our Alfred's dead and that's it. Knowing for certain hurts, but it's better than not-knowing forever. But that he managed to bring a child into this world before he died, that's a real gift. I only hope that Martha stays here with us."

"She's young and I'm sure she'll want to get married again. She seems to like Emil. Why not? But I just can't stand the thought of giving back little Fred again."

"If we were better off, Emil could stay with us. But the farm doesn't provide a good living. It's hardly enough."

"We have to think of something. If Martha leaves with Fred, I'll die of sorrow."

Emil Litke visited the farm once a week. He was becoming quite a welcome guest at Martha's parents-in-law. He came again today. What he had to share, however, didn't give them cause for hope. After the turnip soup was eaten, everyone sat around the kitchen table chatting.

Emil said: “Our relatives are really kind people, but we can’t live off them any longer. They would never mention it, but supplies have run short, and it’s hard to find work here. Nobody’s hiring, not even as a farmhand working only for his daily bread. I think we should set off for Pomerania. We’ve received a letter from my uncle today. He believes there’ll be enough work very soon. We only need to be there at the right time when the fields are ready to be tilled and the cows are calving. There’ll be enough to do then.”

Then, all was silent around the table.

In the evening, when Martha sat together with her parents-in-law and Emilie, Rosina started to speak: “Martha, you are a young and pretty woman. Our son, your husband, has been dead for about a year now, and you can’t be a mourning widow for the rest of your life. I’ve noticed that you like Emil. And judging by the way he looks at you, there’s no doubt how he feels about you.”

Martha opened her mouth to speak, but Rosina gestured and kept on talking: “If you want to go with Emil, we wouldn’t reproach you for it. On the contrary, we would be glad to see you happy and with a future.”

Tears came into Martha’s eyes, but Rosina still kept on talking: “There’s only one favour I’d like to ask you; please leave little Fred here with us for a while. At least until you have your feet on the firm ground in Pomerania. You know how much I idolize the little lad. He’s the apple of my eye. There’s nothing in the world I wouldn’t do for him.”

Volhynia 1920

– 33 –

"Of course, madam shithead!" said Katlika, after her *mistress* who sat at the dining table had given her some instructions. Katlika spoke Polish with the lady of the house.

"What does shithead mean?" she asked.

"Oh, it's only a German expression for *her ladyship*."

"I should hope so; watch out!"

Her ladyship had been gracious enough to permit Katlika and her mother to stay at her parental home, which actually belonged to Christine. However, de facto it didn't. They were allowed to live in a small chamber in their own house on condition that both women kept the house for her. This included cooking, serving, gardening and everything else Madam Sziszkewitz considered herself too good for. The lady acted as if everything belonged to her: the house including all the household goods, the property as well as the fields which hadn't been cultivated for years. Her husband was an officer in the Polish army which, despite all peace negotiations, was still fighting against Russia.

Against which Russia, nobody really know. Was it against the Reds or the Whites, or some special force of mercenaries. In this time of change and new beginnings, everybody wanted a piece of the action. Things were completely chaotic. The Polish army had advanced up to Kiev, while the Russians tried to lay siege to Warsaw. They were forced back into White Russia by the Poles, and up to one hundred and fifty thousand Russian soldiers died. All this while the great World War was officially over and Poland, under foreign rule for such a long time, was again an independent state.

In the meantime, in Volhynia, and not only there, people were starving. Because little had been planted, harvests were very poor when the Siberian exiles returned home. In the first half of 1919, more people died than in the previous years in Siberia, even more than had fallen victim to the Spanish flu and other diseases on the return journey. The black market was thriving, since there was nothing else left to buy. And, what was available on the black market, destroyed the people even more. There was talk of human flesh being sold, and of people wanting, or needing, to believe that it was the meat of animals. The dying finally came to an end when the home-comers re-established some kind of a routine, fixing their gardens and homes and recultivating the fields for the summer. Whatever they harvested didn't belong to them, but, of course, they appropriated a part to themselves and their families. Now, one year later, the situation was somewhat stable again. But no one ever really had enough to eat. Above all, there was still a shortage of livestock, which had been seized during the war years to feed the soldiers. And, the next famine, spreading out in all directions from South Russia, was already advancing.

After being under Russian rule for one hundred and twenty-eight years, this part of Volhynia was now in Polish hands as attested in the Treaty of Versailles. There was no longer a Russian authority here, but there was no Polish one either, to deal with the most urgent current issues. Law and order receded into the far distance. Everybody acted on their own discretion hoping to make it. The Germans weren't doing well. They had low cultural status during these times. Other people were living in their houses. One had to be satisfied to get accommodation in one of the stables. Some families of twelve shared a single room in their former houses. The hope that things would eventually get better began to fade. Whoever could afford it, left for Germany. For many, life there wasn't much better. Many parts of Europe had been impoverished by war.

Some people left immediately in 1919 when they saw the wretched state of their homeland. Some went to Germany, others to America, Canada, Brazil or Argentina. Families one had known for a lifetime or had even been sort of related to, like the Jasters, the Rolfes, the Hinzes, the Schinklers, the Fuersts, had moved away. Hanna, a daughter of Emil Gehrmann, had married a son of the Jasters family who had been an officer in the Russian army. Having survived the war, he and his wife went to Germany, but things didn't go well there. After a few years, they finally moved to Manitoba, Canada, where many former friends already had got a foothold. Also being a war survivor, Rudolf Rattai made up his mind to leave Volhynia. After waiting for his wife to return from exile in the far north, he was over the moon to be able to embrace his Pauline again. But things couldn't go on this way. Their goal was now Saskatchewan. Friends and relatives wrote enticing descriptions of the land and even sent money for the trip.

"Pauline," Rudolf said one day as they ate their soup consisting only of water and boiled roots, "I don't want to be a farm-hand on my own farm. And I can't just stand by and watch our children starve. There's nothing for us on this land. We'll take the money our relatives have sent us, make our way through to Danzig and try to board a ship to Hamburg or Bremen. And then we'll cross the ocean for Canada."

Pauline, thin and emaciated, pressed Rudolf's hand and said: "I never dreamed that one day I would make such a long journey. But, after surviving those dreadful trips to the north and back, nothing can scare me. I don't care how long it takes or how arduous it will be. It can't be worse than it is here."

Everybody thought about leaving. However, many didn't have the strength or the necessary means. The Canadian government was still recruiting; especially craftsmen and farmers from Eastern Europe. The eccentric climate of the prairies kept the area sparsely settled, and more people were needed to facilitate a reasonable infrastructure. There were offers to advance the money for the voyage as a loan. Other proposals offered free or inexpensive land, as long as they would cultivate it. But, with everything in turmoil, not every Volhynian village heard about such opportunities.

Katlika wasn't too optimistic about her future. She had lost her husband, and her children didn't make it in the north, either. Others had snatched the house she and Eduard once lived in. She had turned from a young and hopeful farmer's wife into a maid, sharing a small room with her mother in the house which once belonged to her parents. She also couldn't see herself falling in love again, getting married or having children. So many young men were dead, lives wiped away in a senseless war, of starvation, or of some disease. Despite all the inquiries they made, her brother was never seen again. Her sister Martha was now in Pomerania, since she hadn't seen a future for herself in Poland. Serafine, her sister-in-law, lived in Mecklenburg and was re-married. Some relatives, sent into the depths of Russia, had not made it back yet. The Hilscher family, centered around Christine's brother, Christian, had totally disappeared. Nothing had been heard from most of the Ehmke clan either. To top it all off, they received a letter from some friends up north telling them that Robert Exner had died. He had been unable to make the big trip home, and instead had taken that final journey that all must take. *Home? What's home anyway?* she thought when she couldn't sleep at night. *Home is where the people you love are, those you care for and those who look after you when you need them.* In this regard, there wasn't much left of this. Nevertheless, she felt good when she was together with Emil Gehrmann and his children. Emil was such a positive-thinking person who always knew the right answer and never lost his sense of humour, even in hopeless situations. *If he was a little younger, I'd easily fall in love with him,* she thought, *but he could be my father.*

"Katlika, did you address her ladyship as shithead again?" Christine asked her daughter as she cleaned vegetables in the garden.

"How am I supposed to address the likes of her? If I don't get it off my chest like that, I'll burst."

"The only problem is that now she knows or suspects the meaning of the expression."

"Then she knows at least what I think of her."

"Katlika!" Christine said severely. "Unfortunately, she has the power to throw us out. She just tore a strip off me because you're constantly hurling insults at her."

"All right, Mother, I won't do it again. From now on, I'll just spit in her soup."

Christine could hardly keep a straight face, wondering what kind of a daughter she had raised. At least, Katlika was a strong woman which was great.

Mecklenburg 1923

– 34 –

"Please, madam, just give me a little smile," said Mr Leonard, the local photographer, with feigned despair. The group to be captured by the camera, had taken up position only a stone's throw away from his studio in the picturesque old part of Wismar. It consisted of Serafine, in the background, her eleven-year-old daughter Natalie, at the front on the left-hand side, next to her three-year-old sister Emma, her new mother-in-law sat in the foreground, and nine-year-old Gottfried, stood beside her. Once again, but now rather beseechingly, the photographer said: "Please, Mrs Becker senior, please, please, just give me a little smile!"

"I have nothing to smile about," she replied.

"Gottfried, please move a little closer to your grandma and stop making faces. Mrs Becker senior, if you can't smile, then please at least look at me. What sort of photograph will this be if you keep staring at your feet?"

"Well, hurry up and snap the picture already. We can't waste all day. There's still a lot to do in town before we can go home. Not everybody earns a living by taking snapshots and talking big."

The poor photographer's face turned bright red, and would have liked to yell at the old woman. Instead, in despair, he pressed the shutter. Thus, a photograph was created which Serafine would send to Pomerania, Volhynia and Canada, to show her relatives who were scattered to the four corners of the earth, that she had found domestic bliss again.

In 1919, Serafine, her children Natalie and Gottfried, and her sister Augustine arrived safe and sound in Germany. Along the long way which had begun north of the Polar Circle, through Moscow and Warsaw, everyone stayed healthy even while disease and death raged around them. She settled in the village of Dambeck, near the town of Bobitz, with the Baltic town of Wismar to the north and the city of Schwerin in the south. The landscape of Mecklenburg from which her forefathers had come was flat and rich with lakes and rivers, grain and vegetables, gardens and fruit trees, woods and meadows. It didn't differ much from the countryside she had left behind in Volhynia. The weather here in Mecklenburg was much milder though. Snow was rare in winter and summers weren't hot like an oven.

Serafine married again very soon. Heinrich Becker was ten years older than her and lived with his mother whom she had to co-marry, of course. This was probably what scared off earlier brides-to-be. Though the mother-in-law was just sixty years old, she seemed more like a ninety-year-old. The haggard face, the stooped walk, and the habit to keep her eyes lowered all the time, suggested a hard life which she never talked about. The black skirts she wore were so long that even her shoes were covered. She moved with deliberate slowness, and when she looked at anyone it was with an accusing glare. She had given her children a very strict upbringing. Even her grandchildren had to obey, otherwise she took the cane. In the evenings she read the Bible, and on Sundays the whole family had to go to church. The other daughters-in-law as well as her sons kept a respectful distance.

Barely a year after her marriage Serafine gave birth to another daughter. Emma was a blonde girl of beguiling charm who would be regarded as a stunning beauty all her life, even as she aged.

In the photo that was taken in Wismar in 1923, Emma is three years old, wearing a short white dress, and looking expectantly into the camera with her big eyes. Her eleven-year-old sister Natalie almost gives the impression of being a young lady, although she is short and dainty, as is the family tendency, whereas Gottfried is just irritated to have to stand in his good clothes beside the grandmother who dominates the photograph. She sits stooped on the chair, only the tips of her shoes peeping out from under the long skirt. She keeps a firm grip on a big heavy Bible as if her life depended on it.

An observer would wonder: Why on earth does the old lady lug a big heavy Bible with her to the photographer? And another question: Where is Serafine's husband? While the first question cannot be answered with the help of common sense, the answer to the second question is: because Heinrich, except on Sundays, never had time. He worked from early in the morning until late into the night and would never have taken off even a half-day just to pose for a photo.

"Good God, that was a difficult birth. That really took some doing!" said Leonard, the photographer, after he released the shutter.

He got a prompt response from the old lady: "Leave God out of it. He's got nothing to do with your snapping."

"I'm not snapping, dear madam, I take photographs." *If the old bag says 'snapping' one more time, I'm going to strangle her,* thought Leonard.

"Please make five prints, Mr Leonard," said Serafine. "I'll come next week and pick them up. Would you like me to pay now?"

"Now would certainly be cheaper than next week, Mrs Becker. Today the photos cost 25 billion Mark. Next week they might cost ten times as much."

"I could also pay you in kind. How about some eggs and a piece of bacon? And, in addition to that, maybe some fresh vegetables? This currency is not affected by inflation."

"That would be the best. This kind of currency always remains stable."

– 35 –

Life in Germany after the war was far from easy. Coping with the destruction of the war was manageable. However, the conditions imposed by the victorious powers were hard. Industry was bankrupt, and the army of unemployed was huge. In order to pay the war debts, the government came upon the idea to simply print more money which, over the years, led to high inflation, until, in 1923, it finally turned into hyperinflation. In the end, one needed a trillion paper marks to buy one gold mark. Misery spread. In the towns and cities there were a lot of war-disabled people begging to make a living. War widows fought against each other to get any poorly paid, hard work to support their children.

In comparison, life went on as usual in the small village of Dambeck. It had reached the point that locals' weekly wages consisted of a box of matches and a pound of salt. But one survived on what nature provided. The chickens laid eggs, the rabbits provided meat. The gardens were full of vegetables, and there was a lot of fruit which could be preserved for the winter. Everybody grew potatoes. In the lakes there were fish, and in the forests there were mushrooms. The labourers who helped with the harvest, preferred payment in foodstuffs. If material for trousers or a dress was required, it was paid for with a homemade ham or flour. To many businessmen, particularly in town, this currency was more popular than paper printed with countless zeros.

Some people bemoaned the passing of the empire. They didn't trust this new democratic system. To them, it wasn't acceptable that the opinion of a farmhand or a servant girl equaled that of a landowner. In Dambeck, it was of no big importance. Here, there were only ordinary people working hard to get by. One could not compete with the landowners in the area anyway.

Heinrich Becker was a craftsman. Normally, he earned enough to provide a good living for his family. In 1923, however, it was hardly possible. When Heinrich got home on Saturdays, with his weekly wages in his pocket, Gottfried was sent to the grocer with a list of their most important needs. He raced down the street as if he was being chased. Sometimes it was only a matter of a minutes before the prices rose again. And it was possible that he could only get what was on top of the list: matches, salt and oil – in exchange for his stepfather's weekly wages.

Serafine's mother-in-law had leased a small farmstead for the entire family to live on. There were chickens, ducks, a cow and a pig which was to be slaughtered in the winter. Of course, there was a potato field, lots of vegetables, fruit trees, gooseberry and currant bushes. Serafine enjoyed working in the garden and with the animals. Although her mother-in-law was a difficult character, at war with almost everybody, both women got along with each other astonishingly well. The old woman had respect for Serafine's diligence and skillfulness. She was also impressed by the young woman's trust in God and the devoutness with which she taught prayers to her children from an early age. Life was worth living, even in such difficult times. In the evenings, when the work was done, Serafine, who had always enjoyed singing, took out her self-written songbook and sang one song after another, while the old lady listened with pleasure. Though she herself kept her lips pressed together, one could tell that she really enjoyed this kind of human company.

There was only one in the family who simply could not cope: Gottfried. The boy suffered from the rejection of his stepfather, who idolized his own daughter, but had no kind words or affection for his stepchildren. Maybe it was simply jealousy. He grew up without a father, his stepfather didn't take on the father role. Moreover, Gottfried was constantly at war with the strict grandmother. When she pulled his ear because he hadn't listened or had given a snotty answer, he'd quickly figure out a way to pay her back, which, when found out, resulted in her chasing him with the cane. Even though he was as quick and nimble, she'd always manage to get him sooner or later, and give him a good clout, although, by then, he'd long forgotten what tricks he'd played on her. Besides, he was firmly convinced that she was a witch.

"Did you know," he said to his mother, "that we've got a witch here?"

"A witch? They exist only in fairy tales," answered Serafine.

"Well, that's what you think. But the teacher has a book where one is illustrated. And she exactly looks like our grandmother."

"Gottfried! Don't talk like that!"

"It's true; she also behaves like a witch. She looks like a witch and she speaks like one – she is a witch! She's only missing a broom so she can fly through the air."

On a summer's day, at lunchtime, the relationship with the grandmother reached its lowpoint. The old lady had ordered Gottfried about on the farmyard telling him to do this and that. It was his opinion that it was about time to again show her he'd no longer put up with everything.

The family, except for Heinrich who was at work, sat at the kitchen table. Grandmother held the big soup tureen in her arm and filled the plates. When she was done, she wanted to sit down without first putting down the tureen. At this very moment, Gottfried had the idea to pull her chair away from under her. What happened then, became a sorry blot in the family history.

Grandmother sits down, but there's no chair. So she crashes down and sits on the floor for a moment; then she topples over backwards and spills the remaining soup over her breasts and head. Serafine, Natalie and Gottfried stare at Grandmother with astonishment. It takes a second before they comprehend what has just happened. Gottfried is the first to grasp the situation. He jumps up as if bitten by a tarantula, darting out of the house to avoid the catastrophe. Serafine knows what to do, rushes off and within seconds she returns with wet towels to cool Grandmother down. She's torn off her black blouse and manages to get back on her feet again rather quickly. Natalie picks noodles and carrots off her grandmother's face. Little Emma squeals with delight at what she perceives as a new game: "Grandma – soup – bump."

By evening, Gottfried had still not returned. It went without saying that he would, for now, keep out of his grandmother's way. She sat in her armchair reading the Bible. Serafine said:

"I don't know what to do with that boy."

"Leave it to me. I'll give him a proper talking-to," said Heinrich.

"You won't do anything of the sort," his mother replied. "Till now, you've never acted as a father, so there's no need to start acting like one now. I'll manage with that rascal. I've managed with you, after all."

Heinrich looked at his mother with dread, as if he was recalling something very embarrassing.

The second day passed without Gottfried appearing. The third day passed the same way.

"Tell me, Natalie, you know something, don't you?" Serafine asked her daughter.

Turning red in the face, unable to lie, Natalie answered: "I bring him something to eat twice a day."

"And where is he?"

"I've promised not to tattle on him."

"Well," said Serafine. "If he wants to spend his holidays in the hayloft..."

"How do you know?"

"I'm not stupid," answered Serafine. "But tell him that grandmother's got a good memory. Even if he decides to hide until Christmas."

Gottfried didn't hide until Christmas. He came to the house again on the fourth day and cashed in a good hiding, and proceeded as if nothing had happened, already hatching new plans of revenge.

Pomerenia 1923

– 36 –

In the spring of 1919, Martha went to Pomerania, together with Emil and his parents, her good friend Emilie and Augustine Hartfiel, her foster-child. Since it had become impossible to make a living in Poland, they set off for a tiny village in the Dramburg district, located south of the port city of Stettin. Emil and Martha got married and Martha converted to the Baptist faith. In November, their daughter Else was born.

Emil looked after the horses of the estate, and his parents, former farmers, worked as servants. Emilie worked in the kitchen and Augustine attended the local school. When Martha was called to help with the harvest, Augustine stayed home to look after little Else.

Two years later, the motley family group moved to Zehrten in the Saatzig district not too far away. Here there were better living and working conditions. One day in October, with the harvest done, Martha found the time to write a letter to Serafine, the wife of her late brother.

Zehrten, October 30th, 1923

Dear Serafine!

It's been a long time since I last wrote you. I received your kind letter and the photograph. Thank you very much! It's good to hear you've got a foothold in Mecklenburg and have married again. To all appearances, you're doing very well. The news we get from Volhynia is anything but good. Everybody wants to leave. Your brother Rudolf is already in Canada. Many other friends and relatives have been drawn there as well. For the time being, I'm going to stay in Pomerania. We earn our living, though life here can't be compared to the way things were in Volhynia. But we can't go back in time.

My son, Fred, is doing well in Poland. My former mother-in-law, Rosina, often writes to me and shares how he's developing. Of course, I'd like to have him stay with me. But it would break Rosina's heart if I took him away. I'm planning to visit him next year. By rail, it only takes a day or a day and a half to get there. I'm not sure if the boy will remember me.

My foster-child, Augustine, has become a pretty young lady. You'd hardly recognise her. She has really blossomed. She helps me with the housework and looks after little Else when I have to work. And my dear friend, Emilie, who's like a sister to me, will soon marry. Unfortunately, she wants to go to Hamburg with her husband. Thus, more and more people who have become very dear are scattered to the four winds. However, when the ties of family and friendship are strong enough, one continues to stay together.

Thank God, I've got Emil and our little Else. I've also grown fond of my parents-in-law. I'm just sorry that they have to work as servants for others, considering they've always been their own masters. But one must take life as it comes. Indeed, we must be grateful that things weren't as bad for us, as it was for so many others.

Dear Serafine, please send my regards to your husband and your mother-in-law and the children, of course.

Lots of love and hugs from your sister-in-law

Martha

Mecklenburg 1923

– 37 –

"Serafine, did you get up on the wrong side of the bed today?" asked her mother-in-law while both women were busy in the kitchen. "You're usually always singing at work. Or did your husband annoy you?"

"No. I had a strange dream last night and it still keeps haunting me."

"A dream? About what? Did somebody die?"

"I saw Martha," answered Serafine, as she put the heavy milk bucket on the table. "She wanted to tell me something, but she remained silent. She showed me a sealed letter that I couldn't open."

"Hmm, didn't you just get a letter from Martha recently? Wasn't everything all right then? Sometimes one has the strangest dreams, but they mean nothing at all."

"You're probably right, but I just have a strange feeling that something has happened."

One week later, a letter arrived from Martha which Serafine opened with a pounding heart. She sat down at the kitchen table, and began to read, while her mother-in-law stood at the stove watching as tears streamed down Serafine's face.

Zehrten, November 17th, 1923

Dear Serafine!

You're probably wondering why I'm writing again so soon. Unfortunately, this time the occasion is very sad. My husband Emil has gone home. He got a sudden high fever. When it wouldn't get better and he was threatening to asphyxiate, we took him to the hospital with the wagon. Diptheria, said the doctor and quickly performed a tracheotomy. But it was too late and he died the next day. He was only 37 years old. Now, I'm without a man, for the second time. And Else no longer has a father. It's also very hard for my in-laws. They were hoping Emil would look after them in their old age. Now I'll have to care for them. But whether I can manage, I don't know. I'm just a simple worker and must focus on supporting Else without a father. Thank God Augustine is over the worst, and helps me whenever she can.

Instead of consoling me, the pastor tried to talk to me about sin and penance. But I told him to save his verses. Emil carried no blame. He was goodness and helpfulness in person. Since he wouldn't stop, I told him that I'd kick him in the backside so hard, that he'd fly out of the valley. That seems to have worked, because he gave a nice eulogy at the funeral.

I must go now. I still have to write to Mother and Katlika and to my former parents-in-law in Poland, of course.

Hugs,
Martha

Oh Martha, my dear Martha! After she had finished reading the letter, Serafine went to the garden where she piled up cut branches and burnt them. In her thoughts she was with her sister-in-law. *She's not even thirty yet, and is now widowed for the second time. Her mother and sister are still in Volhynia, her son is in Poland, Emilie, her best friend, is in Hamburg and I am here in Mecklenburg. She has only her parents-in-law. And they're not that young anymore. They probably won't manage without Martha's help.*

Just then, the grandmother came into the garden.

"You're worrying about Martha," she said.

"Yes, I am. She could well use help right now. She's all alone having to care for both her child and her parents-in-law. Moreover, I doubt she's earning enough money. I don't know how she's going to manage all this."

"Life is cruel sometimes. Nevertheless, there's always a way. Just ask her whether she wants to come here. It makes no difference if she works on a farm in Pomerania or here."

"But I don't know what the story is with her parents-in-law. I get the impression they can hardly work any more and need help."

"She won't be able to help them on her own. Tell her to bring them along and care for them here. At least here she has you."

It was rare for her mother-in-law to talk to her like this. Behind the hard surface, there was a soft centre, that no one would suspect. Though she didn't know Martha at all, she felt sympathy for her, because she realized how deeply her plight affected her daughter-in-law.

GERMANY 2003

– 38 –

Sometimes one has strange ideas. Driven by some sort of impulse, one deals with a matter one hasn't thought about before or, at least, hasn't paid much attention to, for many years. In 2003, I found myself thinking about my father's birthplace which I'd discovered in an old certificate. Just by reading its name, I was able to recall certain childhood memories. The place: Janowka-Solomiak, Ukraine. An internet search results in more than a dozen different places called Janowka in Ukraine alone, and substantially more throughout the Russian empire. In addition to these, there are several places with the same name which were deserted long ago. Moreover, many places, especially in Ukraine, have been renamed over the course of history. Therefore, the name of the second place, Solomiak, was a big help because it was rarely used. In any case, I was able to find out relatively quickly that the village of Janowka I'd been looking for is located in western Ukraine, in Volhynia, and once was called Johannesdorf or Johannisdorf. Later names included Janiewka, Janowka, Janufke, and today, finally, in Ukrainian – Ivanivka. I also discovered that there are two genealogical associations engaged in research into Volhynia. One has its headquarter in Germany, the other one in Canada. On their websites, I became aware of a genealogist named Miles Ertman who has been specializing in Janowka and Solomiak. From his email address, I concluded he lived in Canada. I wrote him an email asking whether he had come across the family names of Exner and Rattai. Then, I went on holidays.

After three weeks in France, I forgot all about my email to Canada. When I turned on my PC to check and delete more than a thousand emails which had accumulated in the meantime, I came across two from Canada. Miles had answered. In the first one, he told me he wasn't able to reply immediately, because he had been away on business, visiting Ukraine, among other places. Having combined business with pleasure, he had gone on a side trip, taking a look at Janowka. He told me it was a small village whose inhabitants, all Ukrainians, didn't have the faintest idea about its history. They knew neither who had lived there before them nor who once had founded the village. There was nothing left of the colonies Janowka and Solomiak which had once consisted of a handful of scattered farmsteads adjoining the village. It was all just a big field now. Also, he hadn't yet come across the names that interested me, in connection with Janowka. *Too bad,* I thought.

Half an hour later he sent a second email, telling me he had just had an interesting telephone conversation with a distant cousin from Manitoba. This cousin had pointed out to him that there was a book, published in Canada, in which the life story of Katlika Exner could be found. Since he had this book in his library, he emailed me a scan of this story consisting of several pages.

Up to this moment, I didn't know that members of my Exner family had emigrated to Canada. I was merely aware that there were several relatives from the Rattai clan, my grandmother's family, who had gone to Canada.

Since my father's death, any contact with our Canadian relatives was lost, because nobody knew each other personally anymore. The generation that once left Volhynia had died off.

Now I found out that Mathilde Exner, whom everybody just called Katlika, had gone to Canada in 1926, as the wife of Emil Gehrmann. The article in the book *They stopped at a good place* was the gateway to family history for me. It's about Katlika and Emil, and my grandmother Serafine and her husband Friedrich Exner. Katlika really did see her brother get killed in 1914. My great-grandmother, Christine, is also mentioned. The exile to Siberia is described and the return to the Volhynian homeland. It continues with the adventurous emigration of Katlika and Emil to Canada and ends sometime in the seventies of the 20th century. The author of this story is a certain Ken Steinke.

Rummaging around a little in the past had brought me to the present, a present I had no idea existed. All my life, I had been a bit sad because there were only a few family members from my father's side in Germany. No wonder, when almost the whole family had emigrated.

Volhynia, Danzig and Dover 1926

– 39 –

The train rolled at a leisurely pace through the green meadows of West Prussia. In one compartment, Katlika and Emil sat next to his youngest daughter Emilie and the nineteen-year-old son Rudolf. Wilhelm, only a few weeks old, slept soundly in Katlika's arms.

"We're arriving very soon," said Katlika. "My God, this is exciting. If anybody had told me I'd come and visit Danzig one day, I would have told him or her they were mad. And then we're even going further on a ship across the Baltic Sea, and then across the North Sea to England."

"And this is only the beginning."

Now Rudolf indicated his wish to speak.

"The most exciting voyage will be the one that goes across the Atlantic ocean."

"I daren't think of it right now. For the moment, we have to catch our ship in Danzig," said Katlika.

In the last years it had not become easier in Volhynia. Life was characterized by hopelessness. Though the first hungry years were over, everything else was lost and out of reach – one's land, livelihood and home. A few Germans got lucky and managed to reclaim what had once belonged to them. And this, only because it was so rundown that nobody else was interested in starting again from scratch. To restore everything the way it once was seemed impossible, or else there just wasn't the courage. The old structures one could always rely upon in the past no longer existed. However, the situation was much better in western Volhynia, which now belonged to Poland, than in the east where the Soviets had smashed the entire farming system. Now called kulaks, landowners were again being sent to Siberia or Kazakhstan.

However, even here opportunities for growth were no longer available. Moreover, one couldn't be sure that the Russians wouldn't try to reach for western Volhynia again. The news from Russia had been frightening. In 1921/22 alone, more than five million people were believed to have died of starvation. Churches were desecrated, burnt down or turned into grain silos. Priests protesting against this were simply shot. Plus, more people were sent into exile now than in 1915.

"Let's just get out of here," Katlika said to herself, and was startled to realize she had said it out loud.

"Don't worry, we're far enough away already," answered Emil. "This is West Prussia, and it belongs to Germany. It's funny though, we're in Germany for the first time and, maybe also for the last time, but we're foreigners here."

"Foreigners!" remarked Katlika. "Yes, of course, we've got Polish passports."

Katlika had to laugh.

"But then we'll be foreigners in Canada even more."

"It doesn't matter, we remain who we are."

One year ago, Emil's emigration plans had matured so that he'd made up his mind: I'll go to Canada with my children. Katlika, who often spent time with the Gehrmann family, was aware of all the plans. She also loved the idea of leaving Volhynia, especially since her mother Christine had died. But where was she supposed go? To Mecklenburg to stay with her sister-in-law Serafine? To Pomerania to be with her sister Martha? She didn't want to be a tag-along. She was still young enough to start a family again. But going to Canada on her own? Was that even possible?

Emil, too, loved the idea of having a real family again, and, of course, that included a wife. He'd known for a long time, the exact woman he'd like to marry. If only there wasn't this huge age difference. Could he dare ask Katlika who could well pass as his daughter? One day, however, he gathered together all his courage, simply ignoring the hurdle of age – he still felt much younger anyway – and was quite bewildered at first, when Katlika, beaming, agreed.

"Of course, I want to marry you. It was high time that you finally ask me."

So, in April 1925, Emil and Katlika went to Tuczyn and got married. In June 1926, Wilhelm was born. And today, on the 20th of August, 1926 they were setting off for a new life in Canada.

Emil's mother, who had remarried after the death of her first husband, was already there. She was able to sponsor the new immigrants. A new government in Canada had made it more difficult for immigrants. Germans, especially, had a harder time coming to Canada. The British-dominated press, the heavy losses of the Commonwealth states in World War I and the anti-German propaganda proved to be hindrances. However, their Polish passports made things a lot easier. Emil's daughter Hanna was also living in Canada since she and her family couldn't make a go of things in Germany. Thus, they wouldn't be alone in Canada. At least in the beginning when there were countless impressions to absorb, they would have a home base. Of course, they didn't want to become a burden on anyone, especially not on their own children. They didn't have an easy life either. But after a while, Emil thought, Katlika and I will get on our feet. If there's anything in the world we do best, it's work.

"We're a real bunch of gypsies," said Katlika.

"Why?" asked Emilie.

"Because we're always travelling. For generations. My forefathers came from Austria and Posen. My parents were born in Galicia. I was born in southern Volhynia and later moved to Janowka. Then, we were in Siberia, then again in Janowka, now we're in West Prussia, and in a couple of days, we're going to England and then to Canada. I'm wondering if that will truly be our final destination. For once in my life, I'd like to be at home somewhere, without fear of having to give up everything again and moving on."

"Everything will be all right, my girl," said Emil.

Having arrived in Danzig, the travellers managed to find reasonably priced lodgings in that proud, and usually expensive, Hanseatic city. Rudolf, especially, couldn't wait to see the harbour, so the family took a stroll through the city centre, finishing with a side trip to the dock area.

"What a marvellous city!" said Katlika. "All these big old buildings. It looks like prosperity. Can't we just stay here?"

"What?" The question shot out, simultaneously, from both Emil and his son Rudolf.

"I was just joking," said Katlika, smiling. "Nevertheless, it's a wonderful place. On a continuing basis, I'd hardly be happy in all this bustle. It's hard just to cross the street without getting run over."

The few days they spent in Danzig were exciting, and also restful. Neither Katlika nor Emil could remember ever having such a long break from working. When the time came to board the ship, all their hearts started to pound. This, however, had little to do with being afraid of the things to come, but rather with a joyful anticipation of the biggest adventure of their lives.

The voyage across the quiet Baltic Sea during fine summer weather was an experience in itself. For hours, the travellers stood at the deck rail, gazing out over the water or watching the seagulls escorting the steamer. On the North Sea, later, it got slightly rougher, but they still felt like holiday-travellers. When Dover came into sight, everyone became aware that things were getting serious. Here, they were really abroad, homeless, cut-off from the language. I wonder if people will understand us at all, thought Katlika. Language, however, turned out to be the smallest problem. There were people who could speak German. Besides, they were surprised at how well they could make themselves understood if they spoke Low German. Many English words were spoken exactly as in the Low German dialect. They had totally different problems.

"I swear, I'm not boarding this smelly barge! This is just too much! Even the livestock freight train they sent us to Siberia with was better. Besides, I wouldn't even do a sightseeing trip in the Danzig harbour on that barge, because I'd be afraid it would sink. Are you serious about crossing the Atlantic with it? Without me."

Katlika had talked herself into a rage. The shock of viewing the SS Marlot was huge. Compared to this old, dilapidated freighter, the ship they'd travelled to Danzig on was a luxury cruiser. Besides, the voyage was very expensive. One hundred dollars per person, that was a fortune. It proved to be a real challenge to scrape together the money; most of it was borrowed. After Katlika had vented her anger, Emil passed her objections on to the captain. That, however, was not necessary, because he was able to figure out from Katlika's rant what all the fuss was about. The captain promised to make the passenger section of his ship habitable within one week. But Katlika waved him off.

The Gehrmann family left the ship and made the rounds of all the travel agencies in the area looking for an alternative. The result? At this time of the year, no other ship was going to Halifax. And that was exactly where they wanted to go. There were many ships going to Boston or New York, though, but they weren't prepared for entry into the USA. They had no other choice but to cross the Atlantic on the S.S. Marlot. So, they'd go to the ship every day, enquiring about the progress of the renovations, putting pressure on the captain. Transporting passengers turned out to be a lucrative business for him. During their stopover in Dover, the family was able to enjoy the beautiful scenery. The famous chalkwhite cliffs dipping abruptly into the sea, the castle, and the constant ship traffic in the harbour. Those were experiences that quiet Volhynia never offered.

Then, things got serious. The luggage was quickly stowed, the ship cast off and slowly left the mainland. At some point, the view of coastline disappeared. They were on the ocean. There was no more going back.

Rudolf, the son, was asked whether he wanted to work as a stoker shoveling coal during the voyage. He immediately agreed when he was told how high the wages were.

The North Atlantic showed its stormy side. The ship became a sports ball tossed by the waves. There was barely anyone who did not get seasick. The clapped-out steamship kept leaking and had to be patched up repeatedly. My God, I'd do anything to be ashore now, thought Katlika, and she wasn't alone, everyone on board thought the same, except the captain.

Finally, on September 22nd, 1926, they saw land.

"That's Canada," said Emil to his family who focused on the still distant coastline. "That is now our home."

Canada 1926

– 41 –

A four thousand kilometer train trip was now ahead of them. The first days were still full of variety, because the landscape that zoomed past them kept changing. Nova Scotia, New Brunswick, Quebec, Ontario. However, then came the prairies, and everything looked the same. Vast fields and meadows.

"I think this country is endless like Russia," said Katlika.

"Yes," answered Emil, "but their fields are much bigger. I think the people here own more land. It wouldn't surprise me at all; with these machines one can cultivate considerably more land than with a horse-drawn plough and a scythe. Anyway, it's a good thing we're arriving now and not a few weeks later. We can give Hanna and her husband a hand bringing in the harvest."

"Yes, we certainly can. I only hope we're not going to be too much trouble for them. Having five more people in the house is a huge burden."

"That, too, we'll overcome. Just think of how we've lived these last years. Besides, Rudolf and I have healthy hands. We'll build our own house as soon as possible."

Thus, the travellers looked forward to the end of their journey with nervous anticipation. The train pulled into the Winnipeg station.

Of course, there was great joy when the Gehrmanns arrived in Golden Bay, an area named after the golden grain fields. There were long hugs with Emil's daughter, Hanna, and his mother. When they'd left for Canada, there'd been no assumption that they'd see each other again in this lifetime. The home of Gustav and Hanna Jaster was small, but they moved closer together, as was usual in the family. Emil was happy to help with the last of the fieldwork. Of course, he also made himself useful by chopping wood. Everything not needed for personal use was sold. Emil's most important job was to look around for a farm that they could afford to lease. This was not so easy. Fortunately, he met several friends from Volhynia again. Everyone had some connections, so it would only be a matter of time, before they'd find the right farm.

It wasn't too hard to get used to their new surroundings. There were close family members and there were old neighbours who had immigrated into Canada earlier. People spoke German, Ukrainian, Polish, Low German. When English was spoken, there was always somebody who could translate or one connect the English root with the Low German dialect. If necessary, one could always use hand and foot gestures. What was different here, was the lack of villages like in Volhynia and the rest of Europe. There were small towns, of course. But, compared with the old homeland, farms were scattered much further apart from each other. Fields and pastures were mostly surrounded by woods. Close to the houses would be the vegetable gardens. And here, more or less everything would grow, like in Volhynia. Except one thing.

"Where did you hide the fruit trees? I haven't seen any yet," Katlika asked her stepdaughter Hanna.

"There are basically no fruit trees. I was very surprised, too, when I arrived. But winter gets very cold here, so most fruit trees don't survive."

"The winter in Volhynia is also severe, and we had the nicest variety of fruit. Perhaps one has to cultivate the right kind that withstands the climate."

The cultivating of fruit trees never really worked out. Even today, eighty years later, there are very few fruit trees in the area. When the cold north wind blows in the winter, one is reminded of northern Russia.

The care of animals seemed a little peculiar to the new Canadians. In Volhynia, every cow and horse had its place in the stable, whereas in Canada there were hardly any stables. What didn't work out with the fruit trees, succeeded all the better with the animals. They were hardened off so that they could stay outdoors even in the coldest winter without harm. One got the impression that the animals did better in the winter than in the summer. In the winter there were no ticks, mosquitoes or other torturous bugs to pester them. The cattle thrived without a stable.

Also new to them were the long traveling times. No matter what had to get done, one was dependent on a vehicle, mostly horse and wagon. The children often had a long way to and from school, too. Katlika thought: When my Wilhelm starts school, I'll have to bring him there, so that he's not eaten by a bear along the way. There were lots of bears, especially black bears. And there were skunks, another novelty for the immigrants.

"How can such a cute animal stink so badly," said Emil after his first encounter with a skunk. Moreover, these creatures were a threat to the fowl. The best thing was to get a couple of dogs who could challenge them, and also make lots of noise when a bear was advancing.

All these oddities were little things one would get used to sooner or later. All in all, they enjoyed being in this big country, not feeling shut in and, above all, without fear of restrictions. Many newcomers didn't even know who actually governed the land. They knew Queen Victoria who had died in 1901. At the moment, George V was on the throne, a cousin of the last German emperor. But England was far away. Many didn't know who was in authority in Canada. It didn't really matter, as long as they weren't bothered and could do their work. Whenever one heard from the rulers in Europe, something bad came of it, especially for the ordinary people. Here, on the other hand, one didn't even notice that there was a government. Everyone was honest with each other. Nobody was harassed because of their ethnicity. There was no nobility, and one heard nothing from the high and mighty. The people who'd been here awhile, married across ethnic groups and religions. What was considered unusual or difficult in Volhynia, was considered normal here.

In December, the Gehrmanns moved to Emil's mother, Auguste. Widowed again, she was able to accommodate the family. Besides, it was only temporary. Emil and Katlika were determined to build a new life for themselves. Nobody in the family should ever suffer again. They had much confidence to succeed. At least, there were no government officials and soldiers who would turn people out of house and home. The future looked promising. Nobody doubted it, least of all Emil.

Germany 2003

– 42 –

Sometime in September the phone rang, and an English voice said: "It's Miles. I'm in Germany and was wondering if I could visit you."

Miles from Alberta, Canada. This was a great pleasure. His trip to Europe was business-related, but, he liked to combine business with pleasure and pursue his great private passion – genealogy. We spent a couple of days talking about our families, and discovered that, through marriage, we were related many times. At that time, however, we didn't have a clue about our blood relationship. Though Miles told me about his grandmother, a certain Wilhelmine Ehmke, I wasn't yet aware that I also was related to her.

In the meantime, a letter from Manitoba arrived. I had written to a relative of Miles, who had referred to the biography of Katlika Exner which had been published in a book. This, Louis Germaine, it turned out, was a grandson of Emil Gehrmann. His father was Emil's son, Rudolf, who had worked as a stoker shovelling coal on the ship to North America. In Canada, the German family name, Gehrmann, changed into the more French-sounding, Germaine. However, the bearers of this name pronounce it either like the English 'German' or like the Low German 'Jermann'. Louis forwarded my letter to his Aunt Frieda, a daughter of Emil and Katlika, because she was most familiar with the family history. Then Frieda wrote me countless family details of which I hadn't the faintest idea. Memories about my parents, which had been buried in the subconscious for a long time, were also released. For example: A certain Aunt Mathilde (Katlika) from Canada had sent parcels to Germany after WW II. I found out, too, that the writer of Katlika's biography was Frieda's youngest son: Ken Steinke. When he was fifteen, he was given a school assignment to research the history of his grandparents. So he interviewed his grandmother, Katlika, who was still alive at that time. She sent him to talk to other people living nearby who, like her, had come from the same Volhynian village. Thus, Ken was able to write his essay by gathering the stories of the by now old people who had found a new home in Canada. Utterly fascinated, his teacher got in touch with an author who wanted to publish a book about these settlers. The book contains many stories, above all, about the people who came from eastern Europe seeking their future in Canada. If Ken wouldn't have written his story, and if it wouldn't have been published in the book *They Stopped at a Good Place*, I would probably never have gotten to know my family.

Aunt Frieda put it like this: "You didn't find the book, but it found you."

Those who believe in providence, might believe that the book was written, so that I could find my family.

Schleswig-Holstein 1930

– 43 –

"Your marks are all good," said Serafine to her fifteen-year-old son Gottfried who'd just presented his vocational school report card to her. "However, this comment *His recent conduct leaves a great deal to be desired* doesn't thrill me."

"Well, that miserable teacher asked for it. I can't put up with everything."

"What did he ask for?"

"Er, well..."

"What did you do to that poor man? You didn't pull away his chair, did you?"

"Noooo, I only did this once in my life, but everybody still keeps reminding me of it."

"That one time was enough. I still start to shake whenever grandmother serves soup. But now you're fifteen years old, and I expect you to behave like my well brought-up son and not like some interval clown in a circus."

"Your well brought-up son only asked the teacher not to always smack the table with his stick. Otherwise, I'd get a heart attack one day. To make sure he understood, I poured a bit of water on his chair during the break. You should have seen his wet bottom when he left the classroom!"

"My goodness! Let's just change the subject."

"I agree. By the way, do you have some money for me? I'm short of cash at the moment."

"That was not what I wanted to talk about. How is your apprenticeship going? Is your master satisfied with you?"

"Great! It's tons of fun. He even has a sailing boat on which he takes me after work."

"So, you don't annoy him, do you?"

"There are others who annoy him."
"So, who then, for example?"
"His grandmother."
"What does the old lady do?"
"She ruined the plum tree."
"How is an old frail woman supposed to ruin a big plum tree?"
"With piss."
"What?" cried Serafine in shock.
"Every morning the old bag empties her piss pot out the window – the problem is: the plum tree stands directly underneath. She's been doing it for many years. Though my teacher keeps telling her to cut it out, she's still doing it, day after day, year after year. Imagine how many thousand litres of piss the poor tree has received in the meantime. Nobody wanted to eat the plums anymore because everybody is disgusted. This spring, the tree finally gave up its spirit and died. It's totally understandable. Who likes to get sprayed with piss every day?"

Serafine started to laugh, first very quietly, then she went off into fits of laughter, with Gottfried joining in. When the grandmother came by, she only shook her head and said: "No, no, no. The world is full of fools."

Serafine was happy about her son's enthusiasm as a cart-wright apprentice. After he had finished school at the age of fourteen, Gottfried took on an apprenticeship on the island Fehmarn. The family of the master craftsman accepted him like their own son. He only came home every now and then, because on the island it was a two-hour walk to the ferry terminal; and on the mainland there was still a fair way to be covered by bus. He was well looked after at his place of training. Serafine had checked out the master craftsman and his family before she'd signed the apprenticeship contract. These were respectable people, and they also had children who were Gottfried's age. She was convinced that, despite his difficult childhood, he now was on the right path and would manage to become a proper craftsman. She always tried to give him the love and attention he couldn't get from his father, since he'd already died before Gottfried was born. He didn't get along with his stepfather. From the beginning they had been cool to each other, and it remained like that until now.

One year ago the family had moved. Together with her husband, Serafine built a house in the village of Cismar in Schleswig-Holstein. It had five bedrooms, a living room and a kitchen, enough space for everybody, even for her mother-in-law. In the yard there was a well and an oven in which bread was baked once a week. The garden was not too small and not too big. Serafine had immediately planted fruit-trees. In the first year, the well-rested earth produced a considerable harvest of vegetables and potatoes. Heinrich was fully employed as a craftsman, and Serafine could help out a neighbouring farmer. The mother-in-law did a large part of the housework, and her daughter Natalie lived out of town, training to be a cook. The younger daughter, Emma, attended school. They were managing quite well, although the world economic crisis was not avoiding their small village. But Serafine was used to taking control of a situation and providing for her family. Besides the garden, they had chickens and rabbits, and two pigs were being raised. Milk and butter was supplied by the farmer who was happy to have such a competent helper. Serafine not only worked hard, but also put a lot of heart and passion into it, as if it was her own farm.

Today, Serafine was extraordinarily cheerful. Her sister-in-law, Martha, was on her way to Schleswig-Holstein. After the death of her parents-in-law she no longer wanted to remain in Pomerania, because she had no relatives there. And since she had been widowed twice, she appeared to have no ambition to marry a third time. Tomorrow she would arrive with her daughter. There was enough space to accommodate them, initially, in her house. And there also was enough work on the local farms. Martha enjoyed that kind of work as much as she did. Besides, she hadn't learned to do anything else. In her youth, it went without saying that she would spend her lifetime on a farm. No one could have anticipated that they would leave their homeland and struggle to survive somewhere else.

"Tomorrow your Aunt Martha and your cousin Else are coming," Serafine said to Gottfried.

"I don't remember them," he answered.

"I believe you. You were four years old when we had to go our separate ways. At that time, it was at a railway station in Russia. She wanted to go further to Volhynia, and we continued on to Moscow. Oh, I'm so happy."

– 44 –

"My God, Martha! How happy I am that you're here!"

Serafine couldn't calm herself down when she finally saw her sister-in-law again after eleven years. After the whole family shared a meal together, the two women were sitting alone in the kitchen.

"I don't know where to start. The train journey from Stettin to here was a strain. But now it's over. I just didn't want to stay there any longer. First, my dear Emil died, and now the parents-in-law are gone too. My good friend Emilie moved to Hamburg a few years ago and got married. And my dear Augustine, who's been like a little sister to me since Siberia, is on her way to Canada. So, what am I supposed to do, alone, in Pomerania? The whole family is torn apart. In the meantime, there's hardly anyone of us left in Volhynia. There might still be two sons from our Uncle Robert Exner, but I'm not sure. I haven't heard any more."

"And what's the story with your son Fred?"

"I visited him again in Poland a few weeks ago, asking him whether he wanted to come to Germany with me. But he feels so content with his grandparents. It seems so natural for him to stay with them. He's grown up there, and, to be honest, I'm more like a good aunt to him. The real mother is Rosina, his grandmother. If Fred had come with me, it would have broken her heart. Their own children are all dead. She has nobody except Fred. For the time being, I'd like to let the boy grow up first. Then he can decide whether he sees his future in Poland or somewhere else. At the moment, however, he couldn't have a better time as a kid. Time will tell."

For a moment, nobody said a word. Then Serafine started to talk.

"Guess from whom I got a letter!"

"You'll have to tell me."

"From Wilhelmine Ehmke."

"Is that possible? Where's she been hiding all these years? As far as I remember, the family disappeared on the way to Siberia in 1915."

"She's in Canada and married to Gustav Erdmann."

"Gustav Erdmann from Johannesdorf? That's crazy! And whereabouts in Canada do they live? Close to Katlika or Rudolf?"

"No, completely at the other end, in Alberta, which is supposed to be out in the west. Anyway, they're doing well and already have three children."

"Little Wilhelmine Ehmke already has three children?"

"She might be little, I don't know, because it's been so long ago since we last saw each other. But, she is, after all, thirty years old."

"Yes, she's a little younger than I am. But for me she'll probably always remain fifteen. That's how old she was when we were separated. Their train went to the east and ours to the north. I've thought of them often and wondered whether she was still alive. I've prayed for them, and now she's written to you. From where did she get your address? "

"She discovered my address in Mecklenburg through some letters from Volhynia. And from there her letter was forwarded to me. I haven't answered her yet. We can write together if you like. Just imagine how thrilled she'll be when she gets a letter, not just from me, but also from you."

"So, eventually, more and more people we thought were lost gradually reappear," said Martha. "If only we knew what happened to my brother Gottlieb."

"Yes, and to Christian Hilscher and his family. One must picture this: The train stops at Rostow-on-Don, they go shopping in town and don't come back. The train leaves and one never hears from them again."

“But you sometimes have these premonitions, Serafine. Didn’t you ever dream about where Christian ended up?”

“I’m afraid not, or better said, fortunately I haven’t. Because whenever I do have such dreams, or even when I’m conscious and have a premonition, it’s usually because somebody died. However, I’m firmly convinced that Christian and his folks are still alive. One day we’ll get a sign of life.”

Now Serafine’s daughter, Emma, and Martha’s same-aged daughter, Else, rushed into the kitchen doubling over with laughter.

“What have you been up to?” Serafine wanted to know. After both eleven-year-olds had calmed down a bit, Emma said:

“The six-year-old rascal next door watched some bigger boys smoking a cigar. To prevent him from telling tales, they also let him have some puffs. This probably wasn’t good for him, and he totally filled his pants.”

The girls burst out laughing again, and the two women joined in.

“And then,” Emma said, still shaking with laughter, “and then he went to his mother, quite slowly, because he couldn’t walk properly with his full pants. His mother was hanging out the washing in the garden when he shouted: *Mummy, I’ve shit my pants.*”

Now everyone was in stitches.

In the evening they sat in the living room. Martha and Serafine continued talking to each other, the grandmother listened and read in her big Bible at the same time, while Serafine’s husband Heinrich, in honour of the occasion, got his cigar box out of the cupboard.

“Hmm, I could have sworn that yesterday I had four cigars, and today there are only three left.”

Both girls broke out laughing again and Gottfried said: “Yes, counting, now that’s an interesting subject.”

Manitoba, Canada 1931

– 45 –

In 1927, Emil sponsored his son Gustav who still remained behind in Volhynia. In the meantime, he arrived with his wife and son. In January 1928, Katlika's and Emil's daughter, Elsie, was born. Shortly after that, Emil finally found a farm. Now they had their own roof over their heads. But the cleared land around the house was too small and stony. Cultivating it wasn't enough to make a living; it barely sufficed for their personal needs. In 1930, their daughter Frieda was born and the family moved once again. They rented a house in Saint Quens with an adjoining property on which Katlika could grow vegetables and keep some useful animals. It was still hard to make a living. Still, Emil managed to provide for his family. He bought some horses and got together with his son Gustav to build up a permanent livelihood. While the worldwide economic crisis was also noticeable in this Canadian province, it didn't have much effect on those who worked hard and had the right ideas. Those were the ones who got by. They felled trees, moved timber with their horses, dug ditches for the municipality, assisted in road construction and bridge building. For the work on Highway 44 they got paid a dollar per day. They used the timber from the woods to make beams and boards which sold really well. There was lots of construction going on, and they also got contracts to build houses or barns. With the income they could buy cows, pigs and fowl to ensure the kind of self-sufficiency that they were used to.

One day two men, whom she didn't know, turned up at Katlika's property. One seemed to be in his early thirties, the other one was a few years older. She had just fed the chickens and wanted to go back into the house.

"Hello, are you Katlika?" asked the younger one.

"Who wants to know?"

"The last time we saw each other we were children. Guess who I am."

"Well, from the way you're looking and talking, you most probably belong to the Exner clan."

"Very good. I'm Rudolf."

"I don't believe it; you're joking!"

They embraced each other.

"Then you must be Jacob."

"Right, but now everybody calls me Jack," said the other one.

"Well, doesn't matter if it's Jacob or Jack. Let me give you a hug, cousin."

Rudolf and Jack were sons of Robert Exner who had died in Siberia in 1920. In 1912, both had emigrated to Canada with their older brothers. They said that they'd now been in the country for almost twenty years. They lived in Winnipeg, about fifty kilometers away. Sometimes it could take a couple of years until one found each other again, but lately, the Volhynian communication system seemed to be working quite well, even between the continents. Thus, they'd found out that cousin Katlika had arrived at Golden Bay, north of Winnipeg.

There was much to talk about. Katlika saw Rudolf for the last time when he was about ten years old and Jack a few years older. As a thirteen-year-old he went to Canada with his older brothers. Though his father was sorry to see his youngest son go, he came to his senses and agreed to it, because at that time the future for the Germans in Volhynia looked gloomy. In Canada, Rudolf and Jack became townspeople, probably because of their youth, while the older brothers built lives for themselves in a rural area. During the war they, once again, got frightened about being sent back. But to where? To Russia, Poland or Germany? Where did they actually belong? Resentment grew towards the Germans in Canada. But at their age they learned English quickly and integrated easily into the new way of life. They had friends, independent of ethnic origin, and nobody wanted to do them harm. After the war they'd requested documents from Russia and Poland to prove their descent. After waiting a long time, and more correspondence, they were successful. In 1924 they finally got Canadian citizenship. Meanwhile, Rudolf married Millie Koenig whose forefathers also came from Eastern Europe.

When Katlika reported all that had happened since their departure from Volhynia in 1912, in Volhynia as well as in Siberia and the rest of Russia, the mood became depressing. When she told about how things had gone for their father Robert in Siberia, about how he died in 1920, there were tears.

"You're lucky devils," said Katlika finally, "in that your father allowed you to emigrate to Canada before the war. You can hardly imagine what you've been spared."

When Emil and Gustav came home from work that evening, they spent a long time together. Now the subject no longer was the past, but, as 'experienced' Canadians, it was Jack's and Rudolf's turn to give a report on their lives in this country.

Germany 2007

– 46 –

Finally, it came to this. My cousin Ken, who had researched the life of his grandparents, Katlika and Emil – and, thus, had also written down a thing or two about my own grandparents – came to Germany for the first time. With him, his older sister Darlene came along, too. Already on the first evening, our relationship was like we'd known each other all our lives, shared secrets and many experiences. Habits, attitudes, ethical values, and all that moulds a character, appeared to have transferred from Volhynia and developed in similar ways in Germany and in Canada. If an anecdote from Canada was shared, it could easily have taken place in Germany and vice versa. This was even extended to eating habits. Perogies, cabbage rolls, borscht, and small buns filled with sauerkraut, like our grandmothers had known from Ukraine, also found their way to Germany and to Canada.

I was impressed with Ken's wish to visit the locales where Martin Luther did his most important work. The ancestral religion travelled with the many generations from Germany to Volhynia through Siberia and to Canada. If one had to leave a country – and with it also the church – another one was built in the new country.

We drove to Mecklenburg to visit cousin Ingrid, a daughter of Natalie. Despite some communication difficulties, a language was found to make one's self understood; when necessary I acted as interpreter. When Ingrid introduced her brood of chickens and ducks, the Canadians were reminded of Oma Katlika. Once a farmer, always a farmer.

It was Ingrid who had looked after our great-aunt Martha, Katlika's sister, in her last years. After Martha had died, she consequently looked after her documents, certificates, photos and addresses. There were three addresses I made particular note of: that of Fred Brandt, Augustine Ulmi, née Hartfiel, and that of Rudolf

Rattai, all Canadian. There also was a photo of Emilie Pohl.

Ken and Darlene immediately said: "We have relatives in Canada with the names Pohl and Brandt."

But we didn't really take much note of this at that time.

And then we came across another photo of a middle-aged married couple which, presumably, was taken in the early 1950s. The couple stands in front of an imposing mountain panorama. With certainty, Ken said that this mountain was in the province of Alberta. But nobody knew who the couple was.

Home again, I emailed Miles the photo. He lived in Alberta and started me on the track of finding my relatives. I wrote: "You'll certainly not know the couple, but as a photographer and familiar with the Rocky Mountains, I'm sure you can tell me the name of the mountain or the place shown on the photo."

He immediately replied: "It's Mount Rundle in Banff, Alberta. And I also can tell you exactly who's in that picture. They're my grandparents, Wilhelmine and Gustav Ertman (Erdmann)."

Now I was flabbergasted. Obviously, Wilhelmine Erdmann, born Ehmke, from Johannesdorf in Volhynia, had sent this photo to Great Aunt Martha. There had to be a direct, probably family, connection. With a bit more research, we discovered that the mothers of Wilhelmine and Serafine (my grandmother) were sisters. Consequently, Miles Ertman and I have the same great-great-grandparents. In the 18th century, this family had once gone from Mecklenburg to Poznan and had moved on to Volhynia in the 19th century. When Serafine decided to return to Germany after WW I, she chose Mecklenburg, because that's where her roots were, and even after one hundred and fifty years, she still had connections there.

Germany 1932-1939

– 47 –

When Gottfried finished his apprenticeship, he left the island of Fehmarn because there was no longer any work for him. In all of Germany, there was hardly any work from which one could live a respectable life. The army of the unemployed grew month by month. The country never managed to get back on its feet again after the war. According to the Treaty of Versailles, Germany bore the major blame for WW I and was required to pay for the reparation. The Ruhr district was occupied by French troops. Industry was destroyed, and didn't really get going again until 1927. In the following years, a hint of prosperity spread, so that, in the cities at least, there was already talk of the Golden Twenties. But then, in 1929, came the stock market crash, leading to a major economical disaster that nobody could stop. As a result, the political situation become more and more extreme. Communists, Social Democrats, Centre and, more recently, the National Socialists. The latter, in particular, ran around blaming everyone else for the misery. The poverty amongst the average people became indescribable. Among the ordinary people poverty assumed horrifying dimensions. The young democracy didn't have many supporters. The social circumstances were devastating, discontent was enormous. The ground was fertile for the National Socialist ideology to thrive.

All of that mattered little to Gottfried. He was young, just eighteen years old, and the world was open to him. He'd come home for a couple of days and, with his meager apprentice wage, had bought himself a bicycle.

"And what are you going to do now," asked his stepfather when he found him reading in the living room, "with no work, no money, and no prospects?"

"Who's claiming I have no prospects? I'm going to get on my bike and look for a job."

"Here, in this area, you'll have no luck."

"I'm not talking about this area. The world is huge."

"You're just talking big, as always. And who's going to feed you?"

Gottfried who didn't take his eyes off the book answered: "So far, I've managed without your help during these past years, and I will continue to manage. First, I'll ride eastward, if I have to, all the way to East Prussia. There'll be work for me, somewhere. And if there's nothing in the east, I'll head west, out to Holland. And if there's nothing there, as well, I'll go north, to Denmark. I'm not dependant on this hellhole."

" You'll be surprised."

"And maybe I'll just get work here or there, and then bike further..."

"You'll long to return to how good you had it here."

"... and then I'll find a little bit of work somewhere else again..."

"Don't think it's that easy."

"And if I feel like it, I'll jump on my bicycle again."

"Life is not that easy."

"... and then I'll find another job."

His stepfather was becoming annoyed by his cavalier attitude.

"Don't think that..."

"And if I don't get a job, I'll sit on the shoreline and go fishing."

"You're driving me up the wall!"

Now Gottfried had achieved his goal. His stepfather would soon jump up and leave the room.

"And then I'll lie down on my belly, cover up my arse and let the sun shine down on me."

Now he really did jump up and, as he left the room, he shouted: "Your mother can worry about you. I'm no idiot!"

"I'm not so sure about that," he mumbled quietly to himself, grinning inwardly.

"Did you have a quarrel with Heinrich?" asked Serafine when she came into the living room.

"No. What gives you that idea? We just had a conversation. I told him I was looking for a job. I think I'll start on Monday."

But Serafine, of course, knew that something was up. Above all, she knew from whom her son had inherited certain qualities. That habit of driving others mad or cracking crude jokes ran in the family. That's just the way it was. Friedrich was like that, and his father Karl had been even worse.

He packed his bundle, grabbed his journeyman's certificate and headed eastwards. Up to the autumn, he stayed at different places in Mecklenburg and Pomerania. Sometimes, he'd work for one or two weeks for small craftsman shops which needed contracts filled quickly and which couldn't otherwise afford permanent personnel. However, he was especially successful with farmers. Sometimes a wagon axle was broken, sometimes a wheel had to be changed. Barns had to be repaired or roof beams replaced. The farmers were grateful for the quick and proper help. Especially at harvest time one didn't need the stress, nor have the time to be plagued by repairs. He didn't get a lot of money for his work, but he did get a place to sleep and, above all, good food. Then he reached the border. A piece of Poland, the Corridor, was wedged between Pomerania and West Prussia. He wasn't allowed to pass through on his bicycle. So he went by train. While travelling through the Polish territory, the windows were shut tight with black shades. Nobody was allowed to look out. Then, with a lot of stopovers, he went as far as Königsberg. He always found short work projects and really enjoyed being a travelling journeyman. He got to see a lot of places, got to know different people and only had to worry about himself. In the summer of 1933, he was home again and this time he found work.

In the meantime, the wind had changed. Germany now had a leader who came to power with the help of speeches and a great deal of force. There was now no more tolerance. Because the short period of democracy had only reached a few minds and hearts, many people didn't consider the current events a tragedy. A vast majority of the population was full of enthusiasm for the new time, the Thousand Year Reich, which had just begun. At first, Gottfried was rather neutral about it all. In 1935, he was called up to the armed forces. He thought, well, I'll do my military service now, and afterwards I'll get my master craftsman's diploma, and then I'll set up business for myself. He joined the air force and was given the opportunity to train in security technology. He enjoyed it, especially when he got to be present during test flights. His superior wanted to recommend him for pilot training, provided, he would sign on with the military for another two years. He agreed. After another two years, he'd had enough, because his pilot training had been delayed. Now he wanted to resign from the military and get back to his chosen career and do the examination for the master's diploma. But then, the war began.

Santa Catarina, Brazil 1938

– 48 –

Christian Hilscher was happy and contented. As happy and contented as someone can be who's lost his homeland, survived a famine and managed a successful escape crossing several continents. Fourteen years ago he found a new home in Santa Catarina, a small province in the south of Brazil. At the age of forty-four, with less than nothing in his pockets, he built a new life for himself and his family. He succeeded in everything he did. He was now able to call a big piece of land his own, with which he could provide a good living for his family. He had arrived with his wife and two sons, and while in Brazil another two daughters were born. He had friends. The only thing missing was the security of his extended family, which – he was painfully aware of – he would never see again, because it was scattered to all four winds. By now, he at least knew that some of his relatives were still alive, and he also knew where some of them lived. He had recently found out that his niece, Serafine, a daughter-in-law of his beloved sister Christine, still lived – and now he had her address. After the many letters he had written to Russia, to Ukraine, to Poland, Germany and Canada, he'd finally had some success. So, he left the November heat outside and sat down in the cool living room to write a letter to Germany.

Fraiburgo, November 10th, 1938

Dear Serafine!

The last time I saw you was in July, 1915 at the Rostow-on-Don railway station. That was the day when fate led us in different directions. At that time my family and I accidentally missed the train which was to bring us up north. Unfortunately, my wife had broken her foot at the market, and I took her to the local hospital. The doctor said she wouldn't be able to go on a long trip. So, I looked for a place where we could stay. Of course, I also wanted to come to the railway station and let you know. But then I had some doubts. What would the Cossacks who were guarding us say? Maybe they would have made us go anyway. Or, even worse, they might have only taken me and left my wife and the children on their own in a foreign city. I just couldn't take that risk. Therefore, we remained in Rostow-on-Don without telling you. I struggled along there as a casual worker, and when Josefine was better again, we proceeded towards Saratow where we found accommodation on a farm. Many Germans lived there. I assisted in bringing in the harvest, and in the winter, I worked in a carpenter's shop. We survived the war quite well there. But then came the civil war. Suddenly everything became muddled. Red Army soldiers in the area were killed, and the village had to pay heavy fines, so that the people themselves no longer had enough to live. Then, in 1921, there was the great famine. Thousands died. To prevent our own starvation, we moved in an eastward direction, far into Siberia. We found shelter in a Mennonite village where we managed a semblance of survival. But conditions gradually got worse. The Mennonites were accused of being traitors because they had refused to fight during the war. Everyone knows that their religion prevents them from killing, and from participating in war. Nevertheless, some men were sent to penal camps and were never heard from again. Many people realized that Russia would no longer hold a future for them. But how to leave such a big country? And where to? When it got quite bad during the winter, a group of us – about twenty people – finally fled over the frozen Amur River to China.

We were quite lucky to have succeeded in this. Many others who had tried before were caught and sent to penal camps far in the north. Some were simply shot. It then took many weeks before we reached eastern China, and then the city of Harbin. This was only possible because of a great stroke of luck and God's help. But that's a separate story. During this adventurous journey several people from our group died. I was lucky again. In Harbin I met a Jew, a cousin of old Salomon from Kostopol who was running a successful business. You've got to imagine this! One travels across half the world, to China, and whom does one meet there? Old friends from the homeland. In any case, we got a lot of support there and managed to earn a modest living. And soon we saved enough money to travel to Shanghai. From there, ships were leaving to everywhere in the world. I would have loved to have gone to Canada. But we didn't have the money for it, and there also was a rumour that Canada would impose entry restrictions.

Then I got to know a captain and shipowner from America. Also being of German descent, he felt pity for us after I told him our story. He could hardly believe all that had happened to us. Anyway, his destination was Chile from where he then wanted to travel on to Brazil. He hired me and my oldest, Friedrich, to shovel coal on the ship, so that the four of us could pay for the voyage. He had travelled widely and told me that Brazil was the country of the future. I only wanted to get out of China which was so strange to us. But, above all, we wanted to get as far from Russia as possible. We thought it couldn't get any worse in Brazil. So, we left.

It took many weeks to cross the Pacific and later the Atlantic. We finally went ashore in southern Brazil. Our destination was Blumenau where many Germans lived, including some from our homeland. I met a man who was about to set up a big apple plantation, a fair way inland near the newly-founded town of Fraiburgo. There, everything was under construction and prospects were good. He was looking for someone who knew a lot about fruit-trees. It seemed I had come just at the right time. Do you remember my magnificent fruit-trees in Volhynia? In any case, we were very successful. The whole family helped all day long, and I could purchase a share in the plantation. We were all like a big family here.

After a few years, when Erich the owner died, I was given the opportunity to take over the entire enterprise, because I promised to support his widow. Now, we have a house in the middle of apple trees. It's a half-timbered house built like those found in Germany. We harvest apples and sell most of them to America. If it's winter over there, it's summer here. It seems people are glad to get fresh apples in the middle of winter. In addition to that, we produce cider and grow seedlings.

Josefine gave birth to another two daughters in Brazil, although, as you know, we're not that young any more. Christine is thirteen and Caroline is two years younger. Because German is no longer taught at the local school, I've hired Miss Olga. She's born in Brazil, comes from a German-Polish family and teaches the girls German, and us, Portuguese. She also looks after the Portuguese and English correspondence for us. The boys are grown-up and also work in our business.

Dear Serafine, I hope everything is well with you and your family, and that you've finally found some peace after all you've been through. Let's pray there won't be war again. May God bless you and your family! Please keep in touch. I'm aware that my sister Christine has been dead for awhile. But I haven't heard anything about many others in the family. Please write me everything you know about the destiny of the rest of the family.

Lots of love and hugs, dear niece,

Your Uncle Christian

Germany 1939-1948

– 49 –

In 1939, Gottfried was stationed at the air base in Goslar at the foot of the Harz Mountains. In his spare time he got to know a young girl named Hildegard. Dark hair, blue eyes, sporty, humorous – the kind of woman he'd always fancied to marry one day. Although the girl was still very young, her parents gave their consent to the marriage. Thus, in 1940, Gottfried lead Hildegard, who was only seventeen, to the altar. That same year daughter Siegrid was born, one year later Karin, and in 1943 Gottfried Junior. Gottfried was called to serve mostly in Holland and Denmark. Meanwhile, Hildegard would regularly have to run with her three small children to a mine tunnel two kilometers away to escape from the bombs during air raid warnings. At that time, when the bombers were approaching the area, one of her younger brothers would usually spend the night at her house to help with the small children. When the sirens wailed, Gottfried Junior was laid into the pram, and Karin was put into a special seat attached to it, while Hildegard's brother carried Siegrid. Thus it was almost every night.

They lived in Lautenthal, a small mining town, where Hildegard's family had resided for centuries. When someone sees the place for the first time, they might think it's a town from a book of fairy tales. Old, crooked houses, narrow lanes, steep roads, even the marketplace is on a slant, and all that squished amongst wooded mountains. A delightfully quaint place in a picture book landscape. Unfortunately, the times were such that no one took much notice of this. Hunger gradually was spreading. The area had once been rich on account of its large ore deposits and the consequent iron and steel industry, but there was hardly any agriculture. However, one can't eat stones. And so, they were dependent on ration coupons which were assigned to every person. But anyone who had to rely on those alone, was badly off. In Schleswig-Holstein, an area which is, traditionally, characterized by agriculture, things were quite different. Therefore, Serafine offered to take one or two of the children, so that they would at least have enough to eat. With a heavy heart, Hildegard gave her oldest, Siegrid, to grandmother Serafine.

"A parcel has arrived from Holland," said Hildegard, when her grandmother, who lived in the same house, entered the kitchen. Hildegard went wild with excitement. She put the parcel on the table and cut open the packaging. Gottfried, stationed in Holland at the moment, regularly sent parcels. In Holland, there were still things to buy in the shops. Canned milk, dried beans, sugar...

"My God, this is incredible! Today we'll have proper pea soup. Come for dinner tonight, Oma. Today is a special day!"

"Keep your feet on the ground, girl. Plan carefully to make it all last. You don't know when or if you'll receive another parcel. Last time you gave half of it away."

"I can't just eat as much as I want and watch others starve."

"I know. You're a good girl. If the others smell what you're cooking, you're going to have lots of visitors tonight."

"I don't care. Maybe someone will bring a couple of potatoes. And maybe someone else still has a bit of bacon. Then, maybe we'll all feel like we had a satisfying meal."

– 50 –

"This bloody war," grumbled Martha. "We never know about whom or what to worry about first."

She sat together with Serafine in the yard and shelled peas, while little Siegrid, who was visiting, played with the cat. Martha and her daughter Else, who was now grown-up, lived nearby. Being widowed again, Serafine had recently married once again. Her husband was also fighting on the front. Serafine's oldest daughter, Natalie, was married, had two daughters and lived in Mecklenburg, about a two-hour drive away. Emma, Serafine's youngest daughter, lived with her in the house along with her little girl. There was no father for the child. One lived in a women's society. The men made war, whether they wanted to or not. All the work, whether on the farms or in the factories, was left for the women. At the same time, there were the ordinary worries of everyday life – family, children, getting enough to eat, bomb attacks. The women had to shoulder everything.

"Have you still heard nothing from Fred?" Serafine asked her sister-in-law Martha.

"I only know he was sent to Russia."

Since Germany had attacked Poland, all so-called ethnic Germans living there were called up to join the army.

"I don't know if he'll ever return from Russia. I only know he'll never let himself be seen in Poland again, not after all the devastation that the Germans caused there. It used to be very difficult to be accepted there as Germans. But my parents-in-law made it, and Fred also enjoyed himself amongst the Poles. Why not? But after this war?"

"This war will also end, and then he should come here. I don't think that in the future one can live as a German in Poland or in Russia. Too much has been destroyed."

"As if we haven't been through enough already in the first war. Now, we're sitting here, I'm worrying about my son, and you're worrying about your son and your husband. And we're not even allowed to say that out loud. If someone listened to us, we'd get into a hell of a mess."

"Yes, they still pretend we're going to win the war. But no one can win this ungodly war. There'll only be losers in the end."

– 51 –

Actually, I'm not ready to go yet, thought Serafine. So *many things are still unfinished. I am still needed. The children have grown up, but they still can use my help, same with the grandchildren. And when my husband finally comes home from the war, he should have a nice place to come home to. Of course, one always tries to be indispensable. But God alone knows when one's time has come. If I must go, then I must go. I'm looking forward to seeing my oldest again. Oh Auguste, how I've been missing you. It almost broke my heart when I had to leave you behind in Russia beside the railway tracks. I've only survived all the years without you, because I knew we'd see each other again one day.*

"Mother seriously ill. Please come. Emma."
Hildegard trembled as she held the telegram in her hands. What now? Receiving a telegram at that time, in most cases, was almost synonymous with receiving a death notice. Hildegard had faced some heavy strokes of fate recently. First, her beloved grandmother with whom she had spent most of her childhood died, followed by her father, who wasn't yet fifty years old. Then her daughter Karin got diphteria and succumbed to it. All that happened within a few months. And now this telegram. Serafine just couldn't die now as well. Gottfried was in Holland, and she wasn't able to contact him. So she packed a few things, told the neighbours she had to go to Schleswig-Holstein, took her small son Gottfried junior and went to the railway station. A slow train brought them to Goslar where they had to wait a couple hours, until there was a train for Hannover. Because military and freight trains had priority, their train stopped repeatedly between stations, so that it took until evening to cover a hundred kilometers. In Hannover she was assigned overnight accommodation in the cellar of a wine merchant. Since the city was overrun with bomb attacks every night, that was a relatively safe shelter. The next morning they continued travelling. Along the way, there was an air-raid warning, and all passengers had to leave the train and flee to a nearby wood. Because the train wasn't damaged, the journey then continued, and early in the evening Hildegard and her small son reached the house of her mother-in-law, Serafine. In the yard played four-year-old Siegrid and welcomed her mother saying: "Oma has died."

Serafine had gotten diphteria, and since it was wartime, there was no doctor around. So, she had waited by the roadside in her ill condition, and managed to stop the first truck that came by, which took her along and dropped her off at the hospital. There was no penicillin. Serafine died, or as Martha said: “She went home.” She only was in her early fifties.

Gottfried arrived just in time for the burial. Since he'd already applied for special leave now for the fourth time within a short period of time, his superior cynically said: “I'll make a proposal to you. Take a fortnight's leave, and bury your whole family. Then you should have some peace and quiet.”

Serafine's new husband – after Heinrich's death she had again met a very dear partner – could not be contacted. It was not until the following year, when the war was over and he returned from captivity that he found out his wife, whom he adored so much, had gone home. After the martyrdom of war, and then captivity, yet another world collapsed. It was only the thought of seeing his wife again that had kept him going through all the bad times.

– 52 –

In May 1945, the war was over for Germany. But the worries remained. Up to sixteen million people had lost their homes and were streaming into what still remained of Germany. Countless people died while fleeing. Death came from starvation, freezing, shootings, beatings, disease and other hardships. Those who survived had to live somewhere, had to eat and needed clothes. Germany was divided into four occupied zones: American, British, French and Soviet. Martha lived in the British zone. But not far away, in Mecklenburg, was the Soviet zone. In the three western zones, things were rather humane. There were quite a few soldiers of the occupying forces who were remarkably well-disposed towards the population. Above all, the children longed for contact with the soldiers. Many gave away chewing gum, chocolate and other things which hadn't been available in Germany for years. It was all quite different in the Soviet zone. The Soviet Union was a bleeding country, still suffering greatly from the ravages of war. The first soldiers behaved accordingly when they set foot on German soil. There were countless stories about the atrocities committed by Soviet soldiers against the civilians. Especially East Prussian refugees reported this. Everybody was hoping to be occupied by the Western powers.

During this time, Martha received news that her niece, Natalie, in Mecklenburg was doing poorly. She was married and had two daughters. While she had gotten over the diphteria, she simply wasn't recovering. Most likely, her heart had been damaged. Since Natalie's mother, Serafine, was no longer alive, Martha felt it was her duty to help out. One day she packed her things, grabbed her daughter, Else, and headed to Mecklenburg. Everyone in the neighbourhood called her crazy. How on earth can you go to the Eastern zone? What do you think the Russians will do to you?

"My niece needs me now. Besides, I lived together with Russians most of my life. These people aren't any different than us. Who knows what German soldiers did in Russia? I'll be all right."

She left a letter for her son Fred at the neighbour's. If he should return from war or captivity, he should know his mother's whereabouts. She hadn't heard from him in over a year and didn't know whether he was still alive.

On her way in the direction of Mecklenburg she met many people who came from there, relieved to leave the Soviet zone behind. Finally, after a two-day walk, she and Else reached the sector boundary. A young Soviet soldier asked them in broken German: "Where do you want to go?"

In perfect Russian, Martha explained that she wanted to see her niece and gave the name of the place.

"Are you Russian?"

"No, I am German."

"How come you speak Russian so well?"

"That is a long story, boy. Just let us go. We're peaceful people and will do you no harm."

The young soldier smiled and took both women to the barrack of his superior.

"Why do you speak Russian so well?" asked the officer, a middle-aged man.

"I grew up in Volhynia where I lived together with Russians. At school, most lessons were given in Russian, too."

"Where is Volhynia?"

"It's in the extreme west of Ukraine. When I was young, it was Russian and later on it became Polish. I don't know who's living there now. Probably Ukrainians or Poles. Many languages were spoken there. And I am glad I haven't forgotten Russian."

"I'm glad about that too. And you speak German as well as Russian?"

"Of course, I am German."

"Wonderful. We can make good use of you."

"What for?"

"As an interpreter. I could enforce this work upon you. But, as you are a kind woman, I would like to make you an offer to work for us as an interpreter. There's a lot to do. Of course, you'll get paid for it."

They came to quick agreement. Martha was to work as an interpreter five days a week in the nearby district town. In return, she would have her living expenses taken care of. And because the officer seemed to be very pleased about the agreement, he ordered a military vehicle to drive them to their destination.

Martha was now with her niece, Natalie, who managed to get back on her feet again. Though she would never be as able-bodied as before, she would live another thirty years and enjoy her grandchildren. Martha worked as an interpreter and on farms. Her daughter, Else, also had no difficulties finding work. In this devastated country there was much to do. However, incomes were meager, and, for years, food was still only available in exchange for ration cards. The hungry years had already begun in the last years of the war, but now they seemed to reach their peak. But it was the same for everyone. And in the country, at the source of food production, people were a little better off than in the towns and cities.

Through her contact with the Soviet soldiers Martha learned a lot about what happened in Russia during the last years. The German armed forces must have done unbelievable harm to the people. Sometimes she was ashamed of being German. However, one officer took her into his confidence and told her: "There's no need to be ashamed; you didn't do any evil. Things went badly for many of the Germans in Russia, too. In 1941, hundreds of thousands of Germans had to leave the Volga territory. Most were sent to Kazakhstan where countless people died. The Germans who still remained in Volhynia were taken to the Warthegau during the war. Later, they had to leave there too, because the area is now Polish and those Poles who had to leave Volhynia live there again. It's a never-ending cycle. I hope that, finally, we will all rest."

"Yes, I hope so too," answered Martha.

"All the innocent people, especially the children who haven't done anything, should be given peace and quiet. We just wander around the world, are sent away, have to flee, build a new life and have to leave again. I'll be glad when I can finally call someplace home."

In 1946, Martha received a letter from her son Fred. It came from Schleswig-Holstein. Fred shared what he'd been doing in the last few years. In 1940, he got married in Poland and fathered a son. Then he was sent to Russia as a soldier which was the last thing Martha had heard of him. What she did not know was that he got wounded there and, by some happy chance, got back to Germany in the spring of 1945. In the military hospital, he was in such a bad way he wasn't able to write. However, he fully recovered in the meantime. He wanted to see his mother now, but learned she was in the Soviet zone. Being a former ethnic German in Poland and soldier who had fought against the Soviet Union, he was afraid to travel to the Eastern zone and asked his mother what to do. He also wrote that it would be best if he emigrated to Canada. Besides, he asked his mother whether she heard anything about the grandparents in Poland. He was extremely worried about them. His wife and child had already gone to the Rhineland-Palatinate in 1944 where they stayed with relatives.

Martha answered that she fully understood his worries and advised him to go to Hamburg and seek out her long-standing friend Emilie Pohl – provided he could find her. Hamburg was so badly destroyed that most houses had become uninhabitable. But if he managed to find her, she'd certainly help him. Maybe there was once again a Canadian consulate in Hamburg, or at least a British one that would represent the interests of Canada. While the emigration application process ran its course, he could bring his wife and son to Hamburg. In case he really did go to Canada, she wanted to see him once again. Maybe she could travel to Hamburg. Unfortunately, she also knew nothing about the grandparents, Rosina and Alfred, in Poland. If they were still alive, they almost certainly would have been expelled and could be wandering about anywhere in Germany.

– 53 –

During this time, even the people in Lautenthal, a small town in the Harz mountains, were starving more than during the war. Since Gottfried had come home from British captivity, he, like everyone else, couldn't feed his family. Even if there was money, one couldn't spend it because there simply was nothing to buy. The year before, Hildegard gave birth to a son who died shortly after birth. This year, Wolfgang was born. However, it was impossible for a family of five to live on a few food ration cards. Therefore, Gottfried and Hildegard took turns going to farming areas to exchange any valuable item they owned for something to eat. Sometimes they travelled for a whole day in order to swap a gold watch for half a pound of peas and a head of cabbage. Eventually, the supply of valuables ran out.

One day, Hildegard and Gottfried sat at the kitchen table and balanced their accounts. They still owned three slices of bread which had to last for two days amongst five people.

"What are we going to do now? The children must have something to eat."

At her wit's end, Hildegard put her head onto her hands. Gottfried had no answer. Just then, there was a knock at the door. The postman. He delivered a big parcel which had survived the long trip from Canada. With a reverential expression, Gottfried cut the strings, and Hildegard removed the packing paper. Then there was a length of fabric wrapped around a cardboard box. Obviously, someone had put a great deal of effort into packing the parcel. What then appeared after opening the carton, was a revelation for the entire family.

"My God, I don't believe it! I haven't seen such food in years."

Then Hildegard was speechless. After the first excitement she began to cook. Everything that wasn't used today, had to be planned out meticulously to make it last for the next time.

"This is family," said Gottfried.

This package came from Manitoba. Sender: Aunt Mathilde. Gottfried couldn't remember her. The last time he saw her, he was four years old.

From the fabric which Aunt Mathilde (Katlika) had used for packing, Hildegard sewed a dress for her daughter Siegrid. She would tell the story of this care parcel for the rest of her life, because it arrived exactly when it was needed the most.

Ogema, Saskatchewan, Canada 1948

– 54 –

Rudolf Rattai had his life under control. With his wife Pauline and their oldest son Rudolf junior he had built up a fine farm. Growing grain was a good business that they could live on. For their personal needs, they owned two milk cows, pigs and all kinds of fowl – not to forget the big garden in which, between May and September, everything imaginable was grown. It was just a pity that fruit trees wouldn't thrive here. But the winter simply was too harsh. However, compared to the hardship they'd suffered in Ukraine, life here almost was like Paradise. Of course, living in Volhynia had been wonderful too, before the Russian government started making people's life so miserable. The land was fertile, there were even fruit-trees, sour cherries, apples, pears. All those peaceful summer evenings, when they had bathed in the river, all the many friends, the willingness to help each other. But all that was so long ago, it seemed to belong to another life.

It was autumn in Saskatchewan, maybe the last warm day of the year. Rudolf sat on the veranda in front of the house and thought: "My God, how big the fields are here. And I've done all that work with my own hands. Of course, everybody else in the family worked hard, too – Pauline, both sons, my daughter-in-law. Not to forget the dear Lord without whom I wouldn't be in this country."

Rudolf followed through on his thoughts, and decided to write a letter to his godson Gottfried, the son of his sister Serafine. So he got out pen and paper and a bottle of home-brewed beer and began to write:

Ogema, October 20th, 1948

Dear nephew, dear niece!

It's been a long time since I last heard from you. I hope that you and your children are well these days although everything in Germany is supposed to be in ruins. It's a pity you can't be here. I thank God I wasn't involved in this second war. In Canada, we only read in the newspaper of what was going on in Europe. Pauline is going to send you another parcel again in the next few days. I understand the supply situation in Germany is still bad.

We've brought in the harvest, and the fields can now rest until the spring. Soon, snow and ice will cover everything. This is the way things go. It's the same with us people. We find ourselves in the summer of life, then there's an autumn storm, and before we know it, the winter sets in. We had to experience this with Johanna, the dear daughter of my sister Augustine. She came here soon after the war in Europe ended, found a good man, had a child, and then suddenly everything was over. Her husband had bought a tractor, and it was Johanna who best managed to get the hang of it. She rode onto the field, had to stop to remove a rock which was in her way. She probably forgot to properly pull on the handbrake, and was run over by the tractor. What a tragedy! Such a vigorous and active young woman, happily married and blessed with a child, dead one moment to the next. She came such a long way, across the ocean. And then she dies. It seems as if the whole purpose of her trip was to be buried here. Now, the poor child must grow up without a mother. If one didn't know that there is a God who puts his guiding hand on us silly little human beings, one could doubt the meaning of life.

Pauline and I are thinking that someday we'll hand over everything here to our son Rudolf. Then, we want to move to Kelowna which is in the province of British Columbia. It's a magnificent spot. In winter it's not so cold, and in summer it's not too hot. We'd love to spend the autumn of our lives there. Not far from there, in the Fraser Valley, my Uncle Gottfried lives, the brother of my father. He's been in the country much longer and has built up a fine farm overlooking the high mountains. The land is fertile and the climate is so kind that the nicest fruit trees prosper. Even wine is grown. A few years ago he fell off a horse and was badly injured so that he no longer does the heavy work. Then, in his old age, he once more sat down and studied, making his fondest wish come true to become a pastor. And today he leads a small Protestant church.

Pauline and I visited him this year for the first time since we came to Canada. We wanted to thank him, because he helped us a lot during the first hard years. It's a long journey. But perhaps it was the last chance to see him. That's why we gladly made the trip. On the way back we went to Kelowna where we visited my cousin Emily. While there we fell in love with the scenery, so that we've now decided to retire there.

Most people speak English there, but that's no problem, since sometimes we speak more English than German. And our sons already speak better English than German. They can no longer speak Russian and Ukrainian. I only speak it when I meet up with Ukrainian neighbours. I even speak Yiddish with some cattle dealers. The church service is still in German, but I think, sooner or later, everybody will speak only English. But that doesn't matter. It only matters what one carries in one's heart. And all people, no matter where they come from, where they go and what language they speak, all of them strive for a good life.

I also wish you a good life, a better one than you have at the moment. Things will improve again for you in that ruined country. God's blessing!

Best wishes

Your Uncle Rudolf

He enjoyed writing such letters because he could collect his thoughts and calmly express what he was feeling. He now felt better after writing about his niece and about his desire to move out to the west. Filled with melancholy, he took a long look out at the fields, noticed that it was gradually getting cooler. So he went into the house. Pauline prepared dinner and both looked forward to a peaceful evening.

Manitoba, Canada 1951

– 55 –

Things got increasingly better for the Gehrmann family in Manitoba. Emil's four children from his first marriage had all made their way in Canada. In the meantime, he also had four children with his second wife Katlika. While Wilhelm, now called William or Bill, was still born in Volhynia, in Manitoba they had three girls. Now the youngest daughter, Evelyn, was fifteen. And the two oldest, Elsie and Frieda, were already married. From the old homeland, Fred Brandt had joined the extended family. He and his wife had two children. A son of Emilie Pohl, whom Fred had got to know in Hamburg, had also immigrated to Canada with them. Thus, everybody in the country maintained a network of old relations which, along with many new contacts, ensured a certain sense of security.

In the midst of this community of old and new relations and contacts there stood the church. Every religious group brought along its church and erected a building for it in the new country. The Gehrmanns, their relatives, as well as many of their friends and neighbours, went to the Evangelical-Lutheran church. The congregation grew fast, and there were vague thoughts of building a bigger church and adding a community centre with room for social events, cooking and sanitation facilities. The church provided both security and a sense of community. It went without saying that the next generation's worship would be in English. The children already spoke perfect English because it was the language of instruction at the schools. However, the generation of the immigrants still had some trouble with it. Emil never managed to learn the new language properly. But he said he could laugh in English, and that was the most important thing. There was hardly anyone pining for the old homeland, because the things they'd experienced there were so terrible. Of course, there was a hint of melancholy when they remembered the dear people they'd never see again. But it was quite clear to most of the immigrants that they were having the best time of their lives here in Canada.

For Emil, this time came to an end in April 1951. He died at the age of 84. In 1926, at an age when others usually think of retirement, he ventured to come to this country with his family. And he managed to build a foundation for his wife and children. *Home is where your loved ones are,* thought Katlika. Emil was buried in his new homeland and, then moved into the place which everybody enters sooner or later, regardless of the places one lived or died.

During World War II there had been some resentment towards Germans in Canada. Rudolf Exner, who had never been in Germany, changed his given name to Ralph. The other Canadian Rudolfs in the family, and there were quite a few, along with others who had typical German sounding names, didn't. There were relatives who fought on the Canadian and on the German side, as well as family members who had served on the Russian and the German side in WW I. Later it would become even more insane when members of the family confronted each other as enemy soldiers in West and East Germany during the cold war.

Mecklenburg 1951

– 56 –

Martha worked full time again in agriculture, and occasionally was asked to act as an interpreter. Together with her daughter, Else, she lived in a tiny village in Mecklenburg. Her niece, Natalie, lived diagonally across from her, with her husband and daughters.

In the meantime, there was a border which stretched through the middle of Germany. In 1949 two German states were formed. The state in the geographical west followed the values of the western world which was dominated by the USA. That same year, NATO was founded as a western defense alliance against the expanding communism of the Soviet Union which gradually absorbed more satellite countries into its sphere of influence. Two ideologies that couldn't have been more different, fought for supremacy in the world which was now separated by an iron curtain. Martha lived a few kilometers away from this curtain. Her niece, Emma, lived on the other side, virtually in the same neighbourhood. After the war, her nephew, Gottfried, also ended up on the other side. And her son, Fred, who in the meantime was in Canada, without a doubt, belonged to the other side. In 1951, there were still loopholes in the fence that divided Germany. An increasing number of people made it to the western side. But year after year the wire netting of the fence became tighter until it was impossible to get from one part of the country to the other. It was only a matter of time before the fence was replaced with a wall and the use of firearms and minefields would stop people from crossing over.

The western part of Germany got support, particularly by the Americans, to get on its feet again, and the food rationing could be lifted. In the east, progress was difficult. The Soviet Union demanded reparations and the living conditions were still very arduous. Nevertheless, Martha never got the idea to move again, only because of better living conditions. She wanted to be with her niece Natalie. Besides, she was used to getting by with only a little.

Two years earlier, she'd met with her son Fred in Schleswig-Holstein once again, before he went to Canada. She realized that this was probably a goodbye forever. She'd never had much from her son, and neither had he from her. He had grown up with his grandparents in Poland who later disappeared in the turmoil of war. Nevertheless, she believed she made the right decision at that time. He'd had a good childhood. If she had taken him along to Pomerania in 1919, his grandparents would probably have died of grief. Now he was in Canada, in the area where her sister, Katlika, lived. Family is important, she thought. That's why Fred lived close to his aunt and all his cousins. And, that's why she herself was here with her niece, Natalie. This was where she was needed the most. It's possible to love and be important to each other from a distance as long as one knows that the other one's doing well. For that reason, she wrote letters regularly to all possible distant friends and relatives.

Today, however, she received a letter which made her cry. It came from British Columbia, Canada. Her beloved Augustine Hartfiel whom, since Siberia, she had looked after for many years, had died. As a young woman she had gone to Canada and married a Swiss immigrant named Joseph Ulmi with whom she lived in the tiny place called Renata in British Columbia. They had a son who was three years old. Now she'd gone home, at only forty-two years of age. What a life this poor girl had! On the way to Siberia her family had died. It'd taken a while for her to regain her confidence and trust life again. However, then everything seemed to turn out well. Filled with a zest for life, she decided to start anew in Canada, where she found a good man, and had a child. And now this life was over. There must be some kind of meaning behind it. Maybe the whole purpose of her life was to have a child. Maybe this child, even if he lost his mother so early, would have it better than her. Definitely he would. It's simply meant to be like that. Finally, she sat down and wrote a letter to Joseph Ulmi who was now in need of comfort.

Hamburg, Germany 1978

– 57 –

"Did you ever think we'd get this old after all we've been through?" Martha asked her friend Emilie. Martha was in Hamburg to visit Emilie Pohl whom she hadn't seen for many years. Up until now, she hadn't made much use of her freedom to travel which was granted to pensioners. But this short trip to Hamburg was important to her. They made themselves comfortable in Emilie's living room, with some coffee and cake.

"Man proposes, God disposes," Emilie replied. "I believe that whoever survives all that we went through, can't just be knocked down. No doubt we're going to get old as the hills."

"We are old as the hills!" said Martha, laughing. "Just look in the mirror."

"We can still have a little bit of fun before we get called home," answered Emilie.

"Yes, there's still some time left," Martha replied as she topped up the coffee. "In any case, I'd still like to finish this cup. And if God tells me it's time to go, I'm going. I only hope I'm not going to hell."

"If there's anyone not going to hell, then it's definitely you. You've cared for others all your life."

Emilie was about to start enumerating Martha's good deeds, when Martha interrupted her and said: "Fair enough. I've tried a few things. I just hope that the good prevails, even if I didn't always succeed in doing everything right and helping everybody."

"Oh Martha, you can't help everybody in the world. But if you save one soul, you save the whole world."

"How nicely you said that."

Emilie balanced another piece of cake onto each of their plates, gave a sigh and said: "But the most wonderful thing is that now we're related to each other."

"You've always been like a sister to me; and the fact that now our grandchildren in Canada have married, is an additional joy."

After WW II, the sons of both women had gone to Canada together and always remained friends. Now the next generation had grown up, and Emilie's grandson Waldemar had married Fred's daughter, Helen.

"It's just a pity that so many have died so early," said Martha becoming thoughtful.

"Serafine died early, Natalie's not been with us for four years; Augustine died when her son was three years old, my brother Friedrich only made it to twenty-nine, and we never heard anything from Gottlieb again. They probably sent him in the direction of Turkey in 1915. If he survived the war, he might have died in the turmoil of the revolution or else fallen victim to the famine. Even if he survived all that, he could still have ended up in some camp or in exile."

"I read," Emilie now said, "that under Stalin alone twenty million people were killed. We must thank God that we escaped from that hell in time. And I must thank you for taking me with you back then to Poland and then to Pomerania."

"Yes, we managed to escape from that hell," answered Martha, "but then the next hell broke loose in Germany. And we survived that one, too. Obviously, we're indestructible."

"Well, I hope not," said Emilie who, overjoyed with Martha's visit, was feeling quite roguish.

"If we don't die at all, somebody's going to have to kill us with an axe one day."

Now both women started to roar with laughter.

Manitoba, Canada 2008

– 58 –

"All that my father could write was his name," says Uncle Rudy, the husband of Frieda, who's a daughter of Katlika and Emil. Rudy (one more Rudolf in the family) is now more than eighty, and one of thirteen children of the Steinke family. All his brothers and sisters are already dead. Some of their descendants live in the area, but are also scattered as far away as Texas. Although he was born in Canada and has never been to Germany, Rudy speaks German astonishingly well. He knows all the various grains in German, when I don't know the English name. To welcome me, he's hoisted a German flag, next to the Canadian one.

"It wasn't always this easy. During the war one would have been sent to prison for it," he said.

But for some decades now, national origin is no longer an issue. Children and grandchildren marry whatever nationality. There are German, Polish, Ukrainian, Hungarian, Dutch, English names; even a Philippine one. Everybody feels they are Canadian. However, if you ask someone about his or her roots, the answer is: I'm German, I'm Ukrainian or I'm half German and half Polish.

"My father came from Russia," Rudy continues, while we sit under the trees in front of his house overlooking the endless fields and meadows. "He only went to school there for one day. When he came home from his first day of school, his father told him he'd have to stay at home. He was needed for work. Here in Canada, everything was different. I attended school for ten years, although, at that time, only eight years were compulsory."

Rudy worked as a carpenter and, together with his wife Frieda, also operated a farm, on which they still live. The farm house was built by his father-in-law, Emil Gehrmann and his son Gustav, and was sold to a family named Rattai. When the Rattais retired, Rudy and Frieda bought it from them to raise their five children. At that time it still wasn't common for everyone to own a car, and Frieda would take a pony cart into town. Today one travels around the property with a golf cart, to get, for example, the newspaper from the mailbox at the road which is a fair distance. The road itself can't be compared to European standards though; it's more of a trail with a gravel surface and leads to the asphalt road. There's no mail service. The mailman would be busy all day just delivering mail to a few farms. Nowadays, they drive daily into town to pick it up. In the winter they must first clear the property with a snowplough just to get to the gravel road.

It's an idyllic life that only gets interrupted when they must go to work. Those who can spend the day on the farm, don't see or hear anyone. The only variety is the occasional visitor. The dogs freak out with joy everytime a car arrives. Even the six cats, solitary by nature, come from all directions to be sociable.

Frieda's vegetable garden is really quite amazing. Seventy-five varieties of tomatoes, each plant cultivated individually, cucumbers, beans, peppers, corn, potatoes and so on... Makes one wonder who's supposed to eat it all. Plus, every August they set off for the long trip to British Columbia, to the Okanagan region, to pick fruit and come home with a huge truckload. They are self-sufficient. It's been ingrained by the parents and grandparents. There are easier options. One could live in a small home in the city, buy fruit and vegetables at the supermarket and get mail delivered to the door. But this would be difficult, with parents like Emil and Katlika as parents. Life's good the way it is. Even the next generation, which is still far from retiring, keeps living like that. Though they must commute to work every day, travel on business trips, have endless commitments… sometimes they break free from it all, to attend a concert or an exhibition in Winnipeg or elsewhere. They don't want to give up this lifestyle. Hardly anyone would exchange living on the prairie for a rowhouse in the city, only because it's more comfortable.

Of course, there's also a lively side to living out on the prairie. When Frieda invites her children, grandchildren and great-grandchildren along with their families, there are sure to be forty people altogether. The same goes for her sisters, Evelyn and Elsie. If only the closest circle of family and friends is invited to weddings, there are easily three hundred people gathered together. Whoever looks for entertainment will find it. In the small communities there are lots of events. Churches, clubs and other organizations offer so much that one can only participate in a small piece of it.

Now I'm sitting here at the peaceful Brokenhead River which adjoins the property of cousin Sharol, a daughter of Frieda and Rudy. My God, what an idyllic spot this is. One slips into dream mode. I wonder why I'm actually sitting here on this beautiful piece of land, far away from home, on another continent. Because long ago the generation of my grandparents had to leave their homeland in eastern Europe. Because it was no longer possible to make a living there. Because they longed to bring up their children free of poverty and repression. That's why my grandmother Serafine once decided to go to Germany where she, for a while at least, found some personal happiness. But after she died, war and a loss of freedom ruled again. She never witnessed the good and long-lasting peace in Europe. And Martha? She went to Poland, to Pomerania, Schleswig-Holstein and Mecklenburg; she always went where ever she was needed and could care for others. At least, her son Fred managed to start life anew in Canada, as well as her adopted daughter Augustine. After enduring severe strokes of fate, Martha's sister Katlika found her way to a new life rather early. Still a young woman, she went to Canada with her husband Emil. Being new to a place, especially at the beginning, certainly wasn't easy. But when her time on earth came to an end with old age, she could look back upon a crowd of children, grandchildren and great-grandchildren who, according to their own criteria, were doing well. She herself spent almost sixty of her ninety-one years in Canada, amongst which surely were many good ones. Her mother, Christine, wasn't as lucky. She died still in the old homeland.

My God, I think, what outstanding women they were! Without them everything would have been totally different. If they hadn't had the courage to take destiny in their own hands and look for a better life, I wouldn't probably exist at all. I wouldn't be sitting here by this peaceful river on the Canadian prairie, daydreaming. This would definitely be sad. Maybe my grandfather Friedrich once also sat by the river which slowly flowed behind his house and reflected on life. And, he certainly must have had the same thought: *My God, what an idyllic spot this is!*

Epilogue

Where is Volhynia? Now I know. After many centuries, this area, for the most part, now belongs to the Ukrainian state which was founded in 1991. It is divided into the three counties: Wolyn, Riwne and Shitomir, and a small part in the north belongs to White Russia. There is no longer a distinct Volhynia as referred to in this book. The wind of history has torn it up and scattered its people to the four corners of the earth. Those who live there today and call it their home, are wished peace and quiet. There's been enough lack of freedom, war and expulsion over the centuries. Many people, from all ethnic groups, have died. Others, among them some of the women of Janowka whose stories are told in this book, escaped with their lives and found a new homeland.

Addendum from December 2019

In December 2019 I received a message from a young woman from Poland. Her name: Judyta Eksner. She wrote me:

Hello Helmut, I am writing to you because I found your book 'The Women of Janowka' and gave it to my father Jan (Johann). As he read it, he quickly realized that it was about his (and my) family. Let me explain it this way: Jan was born in Kostopol (Volhynia) in 1940. His father's name was Bogumil which means Gottlieb in German. His father was Gottlieb, who is associated with Janowka in your book. Another part of the family lived near Janowka, in Natalia. My father also told me that our name Exner was changed to Eksner after World War II …

It was now clear to me that Gottlieb, the brother of my grandfather Friedrich who had been missing since 1918, had survived. Judyta and her brother, who is also called Bogumil, made contact with her father Jan, who informed me about the gaps in the family history. Accordingly, Gottlieb did return to his Volhynian homeland from World War I, in which he had served as a Russian soldier, when most of his relatives had already emigrated: to Germany, Canada or South America. With his wife Anna Guse he raised four sons and a daughter. In 1943 the family, like all Germans in the region, was relocated to the Warthegau due to the Hitler-Stalin pact. They lived in the city of Rzepin. In 1945 Gottlieb wanted to go back to Volhynia with some of his children, which they considered their home. On the way, Gottlieb's eldest son Alexander was arrested by the Soviet authorities and sentenced to twenty years of forced labor.

In the end, all of Gottlieb's descendants lived in Poland and he himself in Volhynia, which now belonged to the Soviet Union. It was not until 1960 that his son Gottlieb Jr. received a message about his father. Travelling from the Soviet Union to Poland was not easy at the time. However, due to an invitation, he received a visitor's visa. He was in poor physical and mental condition, but never told what had happened to him in the years since 1945. He did not return to Volhynia, but stayed in Poland with his children. A few years later he died in a village near Wroclaw (Breslau).

This closes a circle. When I started researching my family, I knew next to nothing. Now I have information about all of my grandparents' siblings and their descendants. The news from Poland was also welcomed by relatives in Canada. Frieda, now 90 years old, immediately said that she would come to Germany with her son Ken in June 2020 to travel to Poland with me. Of course we wanted to get to know this newly discovered branch of our clan at a family get-together across countries and continents. Then Corona came and we had to postpone our plans. But after it took us over a hundred years to get back together, we will probably survive the pandemic too, in order to finally face each other after generations. Family is an incredibly strong bond. Our ancestors proved it, and we will accomplish it.

There are stories that one can't finish telling because they aren't over. It's impossible to draw an appropriate conclusion to every character mentioned in a book such as this. Nevertheless, one wants to know what happened to the people we got to know here:

Helmut Exner, youngest son of Gottfried and Hildegard, grandson of Serafine and Friedrich, wrote this book. He lives in Lower Saxony with his family and runs a small publishing house. Learning about his family history and then re-establishing contact with a large number of his relatives, means a lot to him.

Gottfried Exner managed to finally receive his Master's certificate after the war, as he had planned in his youth. He continued to live in the Harz region with his family, where he and his wife **Hildegard** died in 1979.

Martha Litke, née Exner, died in 1988 at the age of 92 in Mecklenburg, under the care of her niece Ingrid, a daughter of Natalie.

For his retirement, **Fred Brandt**, Martha's son, moved from Manitoba to British Columbia where he later died.

Mathilde (Katlika) Gehrmann, née Exner, widowed Ehmke, died in 1985 at the age of 91 in Manitoba. She left behind four children, seventeen grandchildren and a big flock of great- and great-great-grandchildren who almost all live in the region.

As pensioners, **Rudolf Rattai** and his wife **Pauline**, née Ehmke, moved from Saskatchewan to Kelowna, British Columbia. Rudolf died there in 1967 and Pauline in 1972. Their son **Gottfried** became a pastor and lived in Medicine Hat. His son also later became a pastor and lives in the same town to this day.

Rudolf (Ralph) Exner died in 1992 in Winnipeg at the age of 93. His wife **Millie**, née König, died in 2007 at the age of 102. They left behind two daughters.

Jacob (Jack) Exner died in 1937 in Winnipeg.

Wilhelmine Ertman (Erdmann), née Ehmke, died in 1998 at the age of 98 in Alberta. Her grandson **Miles**, the most important genealogist in the family, lives in Edmonton and is a world-renowned photographer.

Emma, the youngest daughter of Serafine, died in 2007 in Schleswig-Holstein.

Frieda Steinke, daughter of Katlika and Emil, visited Germany in 2017. She died in Beausejour in 2021 at the age of 91.

What became of **Christian Hilscher** and his family has not yet been researched.

Some relatives who didn't succeed in escaping from Volhynia after WW I were resettled to the Warthegau during WW II. At the end of the war, they had to leave this region again to make room for the Poles who were expelled from Volhynia by the Soviets.

Other relatives didn't return from their *excursion* to Siberia. Some still live in the Orenburg region. During the Stalin era, these people had to carry the heavy burden of being ethnic Germans: Resettlement to Kazahkstan or to east Siberia, labour camps, ban of religion and a variety of harassments invented to suppress others. It was not until the Breschnev era that some permissiveness set in, e.g. the limited freedom of choosing one's domicile.

The main characters in this book

Augustine Hartfiel
Friend / foster-child of Martha Exner

Christian Hilscher
Brother of Christine Exner

Christine Exner, geb. Hilscher
Farmer's wife in Volhynia, married to Karl Exner, mother of Friedrich, Gottlieb, Mathilde (Katlika) and Martha, great-grandmother of Helmut Exner

Eduard Ehmke
The first husband of Mathilde (Katlika)

Emil Gehrmann
Friend and neighbour of the Exner family, later Katlika's husband

Emilie Pohl
Friend of Martha Exner

Fred Brandt junior
Son of Martha Exner

Friedrich Exner
Husband of Serafine, son of Christine and Karl Exner, grandfather of Helmut Exner

Gottfried Exner
Son of Serafine and Friedrich Exner, father of Helmut Exner

Gottlieb Exner

Son of Christine and Karl Exner

Helmut Exner

Author / narrator of this book

Jacob (Jack) Exner

Son of Robert Exner, brother of Rudolf Exner

Karl Exner

Farmer in Volhynia, married to Christine, father of Friedrich, Gottlieb, Mathilde (Katlika) and Martha, great-grandfather of Helmut Exner

Karl Rattai

Father of Serafine and Rudolf, married to Pauline Rattai Senior, née Ehmke, great-grandfather of Helmut Exner

Ken Steinke

Cousin of Helmut Exner, grandchild of Emil and Mathilde (Katlika)

Martha Exner

Daughter of Christine and Karl Exner

Mathilde (Katlika) Exner

Daughter of Christine and Karl Exner

Miles Ertman

Grandson of Wilhelmine Ehmke

Natalie Exner

Daughter of Serafine und Friedrich Exner

Pauline Rattai senior, neé Ehmke
Wife of Karl Rattai, mother of Rudolf and Serafine, great-grandmother of Helmut Exner

Pauline Rattai junior, neé Ehmke
Wife of Rudolf Rattai

Robert Exner
Cloth manufacturer in Rozyscsze, brother of Karl Exner, father of Rudolf (Ralph) and Jacob (Jack) Exner

Rudolf (Ralph) Exner
Son of Robert Exner

Rudolf Rattai
Married to Pauline Ehmke junior, son of Pauline Rattai Senior and Karl Rattai, brother of Serafine Exner

Serafine Exner
Married to Friedrich Exncr, daughter of Karl and Pauline Rattai Senior, grandmother of Helmut Exner

Wilhelmine Ehmke
Cousin of Serafine, grandmother of Miles

Appendix

Taken in Wismar, Germany, in 1923:
Serafine at the back;
in front (from the left to the right):
Natalie, Emma, Grandmother Becker, Gottfried

Friedrich Exner in Volhynia, 1914

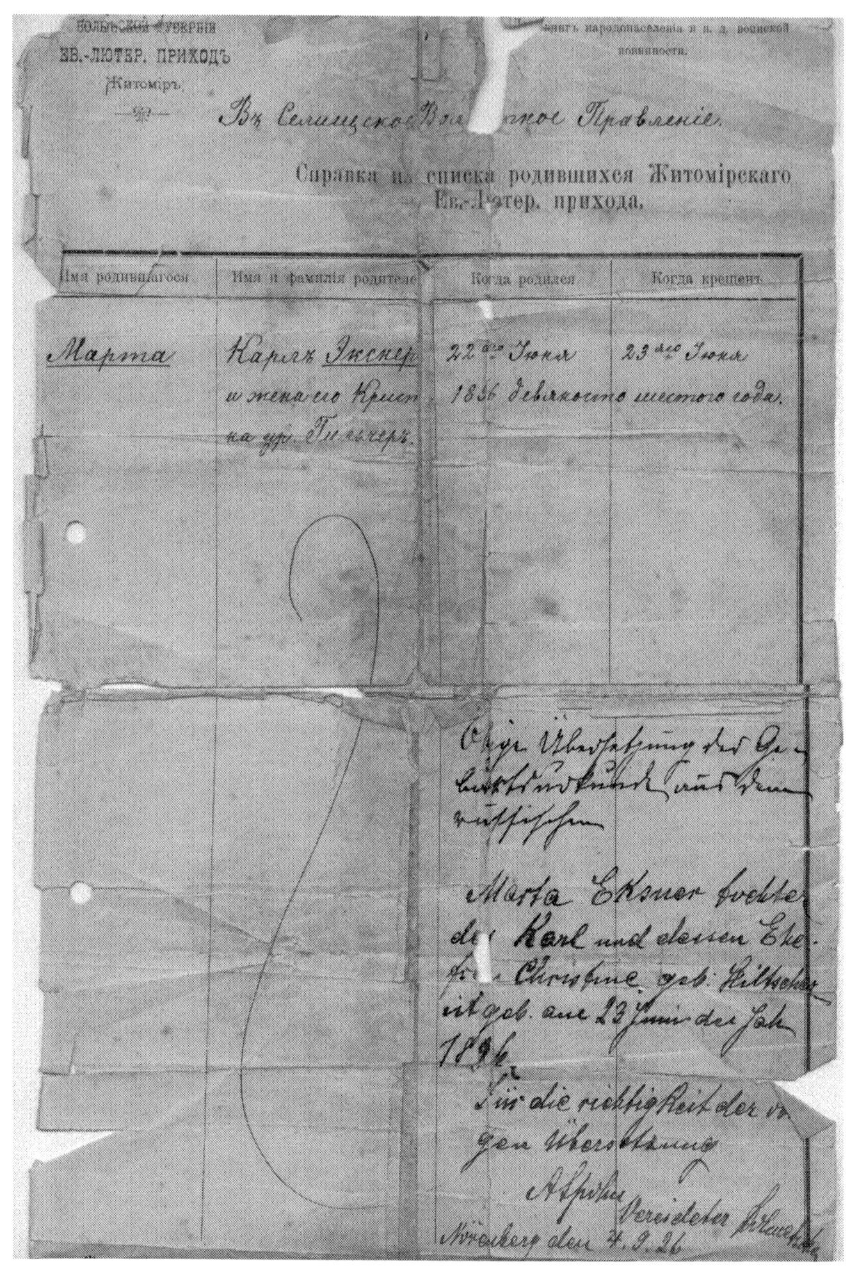

Волынской губерніи
ЕВ.-ЛЮТЕР. ПРИХОДЪ
Житоміръ

...книгъ народонаселенія и п. д. воинской повинности.

Въ Селищское Волостное Правленіе.

Справка изъ списка родившихся Житомірскаго Ев.-Лютер. прихода.

Имя родившагося	Имя и фамилія родителей	Когда родился	Когда крещенъ
Марта	Карлъ Экснеръ и жена его Христина ур. Гильхеръ	22-го Іюня 1896 девяносто шестого года	23-го Іюня

Copie Übersetzung der Geburtsurkunde aus dem russischen

Marta Eksner Tochter des Karl und dessen Ehefrau Christine geb. Hiltscher ist geb. am 23 Juni des Jahr 1896.

Für die Richtigkeit der vorliegenden Übersetzung

[illegible]
Vereidigter Übersetzer

Nürnberg den 4.9.26

Birth certificate of Martha Exner

Above: The home of the Rattais in the Fraser Valley, British Columbia, in the 1920s.

Left: Gustav and Wilhelmine Erdmann in Banff, Alberta, in the 1950s

Rudolf (Ralph) Exner and his wife Millie
in front of their house in Winnipeg

Harvest in Manitoba:
Mathilde (Katlika) with her daughters Evelyn and Elsie

Emil Gehrmann
with his horses in Manitoba

Hamburg, Germany, 1978:
Martha (left) visits her friend Emilie Pohl (middle)

Martha on her 90th birthday

The church in Dambeck, Mecklenburg, Germany
(photos: P. Barsch)

Lautenthal, Germany:
View of the market place

Lautenthal, Germany:
View of the house where the Exner family lived

Hildegard Exner with her daughters
Karin and Siegrid (1943)

Central Europe 1914

The approximate route from Volhynia to the exile on the Jamal Peninsula, North Siberia, is drawn in on the map.

British
Columbia
Alberta
Edmonton
Kelowna
Fraser Valley
Saskatche -
wan
Manitoba
Ogema
Winnipeg
Halifax

Canada

About the author

My name is Helmut Exner and I was born in Lautenthal, a cosy little town in the Harz Mountains, in 1953. Writing is a big passion of mine which I have always been pursuing, but without placing great importance on my name to appear.

My first novel, *The Women of Janowka*, a review of my own family history, was published in 2010. Still, I've been receiving letters and messages from all over the world from people who have read the book. As a result, this *true story* has also been published in English. However, books like this can only be written once in a lifetime, because it's a matter of the heart.

I am better known for my cozy-crime novels, which mainly take place in the Harz Mountains, featuring the occasional use of the coarse language of the region and odd characters. It is the mixture of tension, puns and a penchant for weirdness that defines the originality of these books. Lilly Höschen, the quick-witted old lady aka the Miss Marple of the Harz Mountains, has become a popular series character.

I have two sons and four grandchildren and live in Duderstadt, southern Lower Saxony.

For more information about me and my books:

https://www.helmutexner.de
https://www.facebook.com/HelmutExnerAutor/

Acknowledgements

This book, in its present form, could only appear because there were people who supported me in many different ways.

First of all, I'd like to express sincere thanks to my cousin, Miles Ertman, from Alberta, Canada. He was the one who generally put me on the right track to find many *missing* relatives. And after some time, we even found out that we're related to each other. A special thanks goes to my cousin, Ken Steinke, in Manitoba, Canada. With his story *The German Crossover*, published in the book *THEY STOPPED AT A GOOD PLACE*, he made a considerable contribution to our family's genealogy. A warm thank-you goes to my Aunt Frieda Steinke in Manitoba for her tireless effort in searching for documents and photographs as well as for sending me valuable books about the history of Volhynian settlers in Canada. That she was able to get a hold of these long out-of-print rarities at all, seems like a miracle. I also owe my cousin, Darlene Omichinski, Manitoba, a great debt of gratitude for tirelessly rummaging through the family's photo collection that she manages. The same goes for my cousin, Ken Wersch, in Saskatchewan as well as for my cousin, Ingrid Andersson, in Mecklenburg, too. Thank you for sending me old documents and pictures. Thank you to my cousin, Vanessa Erkelens, for the photos of the Brokenhead River.

A special thank-you goes to my wife, Ursula Exner, who read the manuscript during the writing process. She encouraged me to keep writing because she had to know how the story continued.

Thanks to the *test readers* of the finished manuscript, Dr. Claudia Raabe and Peter Zastrow. Their words of advice were of great value to me. A big thank-you goes to my friend and adviser who also happens to be my son: Sascha Exner. His competent advice and his feeling for language are everything an author could wish for.

At this point, I'd also like to thank a society which, as a non-profit-making organization, does an excellent job supporting the work of many genealogists: the *SGGEE Society for German Genealogy in Eastern Europe*. A big thank-you also goes to Irene and Gerhard König for their commitment to run the website WWW.WOLHYNIEN.DE, which has helped a lot of genealogists make decisive progress.

For the realization of the English version of this book, I'd like express my most sincere gratitude to Sascha Exner, Gabriele Goldstone and Ken Steinke.

The River Slusz near Janowka (photo: Miles Ertman)

The Brokenhead River near Beausejour, Manitoba
(photo: Vanessa Erkelens)

Printed in Poland
by Amazon Fulfillment
Poland Sp. z o.o., Wrocław

79875508R00127